E. H. Plumptre

Lazarus and other poems by E. H. Plumptre

Fourth edition

E. H. Plumptre

Lazarus and other poems by E. H. Plumptre
Fourth edition

ISBN/EAN: 9783743333697

Manufactured in Europe, USA, Canada, Australia, Japa

Cover: Foto ©Andreas Hilbeck / pixelio.de

Manufactured and distributed by brebook publishing software
(www.brebook.com)

E. H. Plumptre

Lazarus and other poems by E. H. Plumptre

L A Z A R U S

And other Poems

By E. H. PLUMPTRE, D.D.

DEAN OF WELLS

FOURTH EDITION

GRIFFITH & FARRAN

(SUCCESSORS TO NEWBERY AND HARRIS)

WEST CORNER, ST. PAUL'S CHURCHYARD, LONDON

E. P. DUTTON & CO., NEW YORK

1884

Dedication.

TO

H. T. P.

Two children, sporting by their land-locked sea,
   Launch their small craft to tempt the changeful deep ;
He carves the prow, and trims the sails, and she
   Looks on, half trembling, lest the gales that sweep
Too roughly whelm the priceless argosy.
So we, adventuring on the waves our freight,
   The harvest reaped through years of many days,
Send forth our ship, unknowing of her fate,
   Rough East of blame, or soft South-West of praise,
Warm sun of love, or freezing storm of hate :
   So look we on, through all the shifting skies,
Cast forth the seed to every wave and wind,
   The dim, grey distance watch with hope-lit eyes,
All trustful on the far-off Shore to find.

October 29, 1864.

CONTENTS.

LAZARUS.

—◦◦—

I

THE sun was setting, and the good ship sailed
   Into Massilia's harbour. On her prow,
All golden, glittering in the crimson light,
The Dioscuri shone. A motley crowd
Were mingled on the deck ; swarth figures clothed
In strange apparel, from the further East,
Bringing their spice and balm from Lebanon
To tempt our western beauties ; Æthiop boys,
Bound for the market, crouching side by side
With blue-eyed Thracians ; merchants with their
      wares,
The wools of famed Miletus, and the dyes
Of Thyatira, noble in their hues,
As is the purple ocean when the sun,
Sinking in glory, flushes all the waves ;
The woven goat's hair from Ancyra's loom,
And silver shrines of Artemis, and figs
From Smyrna's hills, and honey from the slopes
Of famed Hymettus, with its scent of thyme ;

                                    B

And strange, rich fruits that glowed in beds of moss,
The Median apple and the Pontic pear,
And rough pomegranate with its gem-like cells.
Jews too were there, the men of alien race
And alien creed, who shrank from Heathen touch,
And ate not with the others, but apart,
From well-filled baskets took their bread and fish,
With solemn words of blessing.   They had come,
Dealers in gold and silver, goodly pearls,
And rubies rare, and purple amethysts
From Indian shores, a ransom for a king.

  They landed and were scattered : some to friends
Who stood expectant ; some to wile the time
In taverns, where the wine-cup circled round,
And song and dance made merry ; some to trade
In the full market, where the dealers met.
But one there was, who, silent all the way,
Had companied with none ; who, silent now
And lonely, waited on the quay, and found
No friends to welcome.   No adventurer he,
With cunning wares ; no wanderer roaming far
To see the cities, note the lives of men ;
But fixed and strong in mood, as one who seeks
The longed-for goal, and slacks not till he finds.
Some eight-and-twenty summers he had seen,
And still the brow was smooth and eye undimmed,
As in youth's brightest prime ; but all the glee,

The mirth, the sunshine of the golden dawn
Had vanished, and a twilight grey had come
Before its time. No curling locks flowed down,
Fragrant with spikenard, over silky vest;
No jewelled fingers played with golden chain;
But plain and rough he stood, as is the sage
Who calls the Porch his master; russet serge
Was all his raiment, and his hair, cut close
To noble brow, revealed the noble eye
That looked with eager glance on things and men,
And turned through all the mists from earth to
          Heaven.
Leaving that crowd, and threading on his way
Through street and lane, he passed unheeding by
The halls of senates and the shrines of gods,
And onward journeyed to the suburb poor
And dark and squalid, where Massilian Jews
Were fain to dwell. And coming there, he asked
For one named Eleazar.[1] For a while
He found him not: they had not heard the name;
No Jew so called had traded in their mart,
Or worshipped in their synagogue. At last
Some traces met his search. In dreary huts,
Where hunger ever haunted, they could tell
Of bread that came from him, of angel words
From lips of sisters who, in constant love,
Had shared his home and helped him in his age:
And now they both were gone, and he was left.

So guided, the young stranger from the coasts
Of distant Asia found the mean abode
Of him he sought for.   Knocking at the gate,
A low voice bade him enter, and he found,
Stretched on his couch, with snow-white hair and
    beard,   .
Calm with the calm of sunset, the old man
Whom he had sought so long, and heard his voice
As startled by the lifting of the latch :
"Who comes," he asked, "at this unwonted hour
To break the usual stillness of my life ?
What dost thou here, O stranger?   Youth draws
    back
From age's death-bed.   I have nought to give :
No heaped-up riches will reward the toil
That waits for dead men's treasures.   Go thy way,
And leave me to myself ; or tell thy tale
In fewest words, that I may rest again."
So speaking, turning weary eyes, he looked
(As the one lamp shot forth its flickering gleam)
At the old book that lay beneath his hands,
At the rough cross that stood beside his couch,
At the white skull that spake to him of death.

But he, the stranger, meekly made reply.
" Nay, father, blame me not.   I have not come
Through greed of gain, or aimless, poor caprice,
To break upon thy silence.   I was told

By one I honour, one, of whom I think
Thou know'st the name, to seek thee in thine age.
Jochanan,[2] once of green Bethsaida's hills,
Now elder of the Church of Ephesus,
He sends thee greeting, bids thee welcome me;
Reminds thee of the former days, of youth
Rescued from evil, of thy Lord's great love,
And adding message strange (when I in grief
And bitterness of heart was seeking help),
Bade thee to list my tale with open ears,
And, having heard it all, to tell me thine."

   "That name, my son," the old man answered
      then,
" Recalls a vanished past. From distant years
Old faces throng around me, and the stream,
Long frozen into stillness, melts again,
And sweeps me on its current. Many a month
Has passed since last I heard it. Then they told
How he, with reverent fondness, lingered still,
As truest son to holiest mother vowed,
With her whose sorrow was like none on earth,
Till she too slept in peace, and then went forth
To bear his witness, and through many a clime
Pressed onward, till at last on Asia's shores
He landed, where the young Timotheos strove,
Unequal, with the dangers of the time,
And there abode. Since then no news has come,

And I would fain inquire how fares he now,
How meets he there the peril and the toil,
The life so strange to one whose earlier age
In quiet passed on fair Tiberias' lake,
Or Galilean hills, and now, when eld
Has come, dwells there in lordly Ephesus,
A prophet to the nations.   I would know
If still that fiery temper flashes forth
Which marked him Son of Thunder, eagle eyes
Now filled with wrath, and now in ecstasy
Of silent love uplifted to the Throne ;
Or have perchance the gathering shadows brought
To him, as unto me, the calm of eve,
Fair presage of the sweeter sleep of death ?"

" What he is now," the stranger answered then,
" My tale itself will show.   In letters plain,
As in an open scroll, is written there
The man's whole being, all the pitying love,
And all the fiery wrath, and all the zeal
For God's unchanging truth.   But I forget :
I linger on the threshold, and the way
Is long and weary, and the time is short.
My childhood grew in Smyrna.   Happy years,
Blameless and pure, the orient dawn of life,
Passed on in silence.   Mine the thrice-blest lot
To call a Christian, father, and to learn
My earliest lessons from a mother's lips

Who shared his faith and hope.   And so I grew,
Not as the heathen youth, who reckless mock
The gods they worship, and with speech impure
Defile their widening thoughts, but blameless, clean
From spot of sensual taint.   My voice was heard,
Clear, full, and strong to raise the lofty chant,
Or read the records of the saints of God,
Or tell the tale, that never waxes old,
The great good news of all the works of Christ.
So bright the morn, so dark and foul my sin,
Falling, as soon as I fell.   The day drew near
When, trained to all the answers which the soul
With clearest conscience makes before its God,
I came to be baptised.   The cleansing stream,
Bright as the river of the fount of life,
Flowed by me clear and calm.   They plunged
        me in,
And I rose up new-born.   With garments white
They clothed me, and awhile I lived as one
Who would not stain those garments by his sin,
Lest he, the teacher-priest with hoary hair,
Should sorrow o'er my fall.   In earlier days,
When yet a youth, I caught his watchful eye :
My clear Hosanna drew his listening ear :
And, as of old his Master bade them bring
The little children, and with yearning love
Received them in His arms, so now thy friend,
With solemn words of blessing, laid his hands

Upon my waving hair, and gave me o'er
To Polycarp, the shepherd of our flock ;[2]
' As one who, going on a journey, leaves
His choicest treasure to his chosen friend,
So leave I now with thee this fair young soul,
More precious than all noblest pearls of price,
For thee to watch and cherish.   Take good heed
Thou fail not to restore with usury.'

    " So parted he, and that good bishop strove
To keep his trust.   He taught me, prayed with me,
And, as I told, went with me to the stream,
And brought me out of darkness into light.
But, ah ! too soon the shadows gathered thick ;
I wearied of that calm restraint of life,
And craved for joy, and fame, and high emprise,
And fellowship with others of mine age.
They gathered round me, and their life flowed on,
In one full stream of mirth, and song, and glee ;
They drew me to their banquets ; rich and bright
The red wine sparkled in the golden cups,
And wreaths of roses scented all the air,
And Tyrian couches wooed voluptuous rest ;
And songs like those which once Anacreon sang
Woke echoes in the air ; and dark-eyed girls
Wove the gay dance, and kindled young desire.
I listened, looked, and yielded.   Bright and fresh
That life appeared.   I shared those joyous feasts,

And bound myself to join, for weal or woe,
The band whose labours bore such goodly fruit :
Nor did I shrink when time stripped off the veil
That hid the inner foulness, and disclosed
A den of robbers.   On each hand that seized
My hand with brother's grasp were stains of blood ;
Those golden cups were torn from dying men ;
Those fair young girls lured victims to their doom :
And yet I drew not back.   I sought to quench
The pain of guilt by ever new desires,
The restless venture and the lawless love ;
And, strong and bold as is the unbroken steed,
I gloried in my shame, and, sinning once,
Sinned on exulting, chief, supreme in guilt.

  " So lived I : and the madness of the time
Had well-nigh blotted out the thoughts of youth,
The holy forms, and faces calm and pale
Which once had been familiar, when it chanced
That two, who owned me captain of their band,
Brought in a prisoner.   Old he was, and weak ;
And yet he trembled not, nor offered gold
As ransom ; nor on bended knees begged life ;
But, like a traveller who has reached his goal,
Like shepherd who has found his wandering sheep,
Cried out, exulting, ' Onward ! lead me on !
I seek your master : to this end am come
Five long days' journey ; lead me on to him.'

They led him in : and lo ! I knew at once
The great Apostle ; saw the self-same face,
Transfigured with the glory of his love,
And heard the deep, full tones that once, of old,
Had spoken words of blessing. Flushed with shame,
I would have turned and fled ; but he pressed on,
Forgetting age's weakness, and with cries
Eager and broken into sobs, pursued.
' My child ; mine own ! why fleest thou from me,
Thy father?   Old I am, and all unarmed
To do thee hurt.   Oh ! fear me not, my son,
But rather pity.   Yet is hope of life ;
I, I will make thy peace with Christ, my Lord ;
I will endure thy scourging, die thy death,
And as the Lord did give His life for us,
Will offer mine for thee.   Oh, stay !   Oh, turn !
Believe me, Christ hath sent me.'
                    " So I stood,
With eyes bent low, and, casting down my spear,
In sudden tremor shook in every limb,
And, falling at his feet, I wept for shame,
Weeping for joy as well.   The evil taint
That poisoned all my life was healed ; I stood
Once more renewed, baptised again with tears.

    " The change had come.   The better life went
      on :
But still I wavered : visions of the past

Still vexed the brain; the snake still slept within :
And ever and anon its venom ran,
Stirring the pulses of the old desire,
Benumbing holier purpose.   Then the gloom
Of hopeless sadness seized me.   Awful words,
' Too late !' ' In vain !' were written on my life ;
And then in my distress I turned to him,
My father and my guide, and sought for help :—
' Give me some spell to bid these visions flee ;
Some charm to raise me from this blank despair.
These hands hang down, and on the upward path
These feeble knees wax weary.   Is there none
Whose feet have travelled on the self-same track,
Who knows the deep recesses of our life,
The hidden things of darkness, and can give
The secret of his conquest ?   Thou, O saint !
The loved one of thy Lord, from earliest youth
Spotless and pure, hast never known my fall,
Nor sinned as I have sinned.   With all thy love,
Thou canst not gauge my weakness ; and I shrink
From vexing thee with all my tales of woe,
The haunting echoes of the sin-stained past.'

  " And thus he gave his answer.   ' Know, my son,
Thy help comes not from man.   No brother's arm
Can stay thee in that conflict.   Yet there lives
One who knows more than others,—one whose eyes
Have looked behind the veil, and, learning there

The mysteries of death, have seen his life
Far other than he deemed.   And he, perchance,
May give thee what thou seekest.   He, at last
Victorious in a strife where once he failed,
May tell the secret of his late success.
But thou must journey far : on distant shores,
Where ships bound westward bring our Asian wares
Into Massilia's harbour, dwells the man
Of whom I tell thee.   Once there lived with him
Two sisters, pure and saintly, serving God,
One most in action, one in thought and prayer ;
But if they live I know not.   He, I trust,
Is not yet gone.   Long since he pledged his word,
Whene'er he heard the summons to depart,
To send me tidings.   Then my lips may tell
The wondrous tale which now the silence veils :
Till then those lips are sealed, and thou must hear
The story from himself.   God speed thy way,
And when thou reachest far Massilia's port,
Go, ask for Eleazar (or, perchance,
They call him Lazarus there), and say from me,
His friend Jochanan greets him, and for love
Of his dear Lord beseeches him to hear
Thy tale, and, having heard, to tell thee his.' "

Then answered Eleazar.   " Mine is not
The wisdom that thou seekest ; yet, may-be,
From this poor, faltering tongue our God shall send

His oracle of peace.   Know first, our paths
Are not the same.   My guilt was not as thine ;
I never knew the danger or the joy
Of that wild robber-life.   My days were spent
In blameless peace and study of our law,
And frequent prayers ; and all our Rabbis taught,
Who sat in Moses' seat, I learnt and did.
Of all the youth in great Jerusalem
My fame stood fairest, and the honoured seats,
Nearest the ark, in every synagogue
Were offered me of right.   And yet I sinned
A seven-fold sin, corroding all the life,
More deadly far than thine, defying cure,
But for the mercy, wide and wonderful,
Of God our Father.
                            How my earlier years
Were taught, I told thee.   In that morn of life
My father died, and I was left of three
The youngest, yet the heir.   The stored-up wealth
Of many years ; rich robes of gorgeous hue,
And gems that sparkled, set in Ophir's gold,
And coins of many lands, and bonds that pledged
The borrower to the highest rate of use,
And wide-spread fields, and vineyards planted
      thick
With choicest vine, and barns that still o'erflowed
With corn, heaped up against a time of dearth
To sell at famine prices ;—this was mine :

And those who honoured most my virtues, bowed
Yet more before my wealth.'

                   Yet One there was
Who bowed to neither: One whose life rebuked
Our selfish quiet. A Rabbi, like the rest,
He came among us; taught in synagogues,
And reasoned in the Temple; yet our Scribes
Disowned Him; for His youth had grown in shade,
Away from all the schools where seven long years
The sons of Hillel or of Shammai toil
Through law, tradition, comment, till at last
The Master of the Wise, with solemn state,
The key of knowledge placing in their hands,
Admits them to their office. He had·learnt
His wisdom elsewhere, startling all men's minds
With mighty words, as one who, clothed with power,
Came as a prophet. And the words were strange,
And stranger yet the life. Not clad as they
In stately robes that swept·the ground they trod,
With golden ring, and ivory staff, and shoes
Of costliest texture; but in sackcloth coarse,
The raiment of the poorest, and the thongs
Of leathern sandals tied across His feet,
So stood He in our presence.

                  And the themes
Were startling that He spake of. I have heard
Our wisest teachers talk in full debate,
And fill our Sanhedrim with floods of speech,

Hot, vehement, and angry; arguing still,
If men, who vowed their substance to the Lord,
Might feed their father's or their mother's age,
Or in their zeal must leave them both to starve;
Or whether on the holy Sabbath morn
The fisherman who set his nets o'ernight,
Might leave them while he rested; or, if storm
Should fall upon his flock, the shepherd's feet
Might without blame go forth upon the hills
To seek the wandering sheep. All this I heard
Day after day debated: but the man
Of whom I speak came preaching other things
Than this,—God's kingdom for the pure and meek;
Peace, love, forgiveness, to the contrite heart;
The blessings of the poor, the snares and woes
Which wealth and praise and honour bring to men.
We listened and we smiled. 'The peasant's son
Speaks as a peasant; grudges us the pay
And honour of our calling; fain would rise
Upon our downfall.' So they spake: and I,
In my thick darkness thought and spake as they.

"But soon within the circle of my home
That Teacher came. I was not there that day:
But Martha to our home invited Him,
As women love to welcome honoured guests,
The Rabbis and the Scribes who wend their way
From school to school; and there with active zeal

She spread the board with dainties; bade our slaves
Be quick and active, kill the fatted calf,
And gather figs and grapes, and pour the wine
Of Eshcol, spiced with balm of Lebanon.
But Miriam, younger, gentler, sat and gazed
At that strange presence, and her heart was drawn
To listen to His speech ; and he spake on,
Discoursing of the Kingdom, and the Love
Embracing all, and Faith that wins the crown,
And leaving all for God.   And she sat there,
Still listening, while her sister laboured on,
Vexed, wroth, and weary ; and at last, with words
Of murmur, spake her grievance : ' Care'st thou not,
O Sir ! that I through all the noon-tide heat   .
Am slaving for Thy sake ; while she sits there,
Calm and at ease, beneath the sheltering vine,
And dreams and listens ? '   But the Lord replied :
' Ah ! Martha, Martha ! vexed with many things,
Troubled and worn art thou.   But one alone
Is needful ; and that one good part is hers
Who hears from me the words of endless life.'

    " I heard the tale, returning to my home :
But still it changed me not.   Some haunting doubts
Rose up unbidden ; but I crushed them down,
Half mocking at myself and half at Him,   ·
As vexed by mystic dreams which stronger souls
Pass by unheeding.

"So it chanced, one day,
We stood and listened with the meaning smile
And whispered taunt, as men who watch the words
Of some wild zealot, when he speaks again,
Still harping on the thoughts that eat his soul,
The threadbare topics of his thrice-told tale.
When, lo! He told a tale we had not heard:
And as He told it, with His eye full fixed
On me, He spake my name. I turned, and gazed
In wonder, for it was not thus His wont
With names to deck His stories. Stranger still,
He told of one unnamed, whose life, like mine,
Was rich in all the joys that wealth can give,
Fine linen, purple, sumptuous feasts and wine:
And he, when life was over, passed at once
Into the outer darkness and the flames
That burn in Hades; while for him who bore
My name there oped the gates of Paradise,
And angels bore him to his blissful home.
But note the wonder of that mystic tale:
The Lazarus who lay on Abraham's breast,
The Lazarus whom angels bore on high,
On earth lay crouching at the rich man's gate,
A beggar full of sores. I felt the sting
Of that concealed rebuke. ' Is this,' I asked,
' The crown of true obedience? Must I die,
I, Eleazar, honoured, blameless, rich,
And pass to torments? If I seek to gain

C

The fair, green fields of Eden, must I live
As Eleazar, homeless, friendless, poor,
The dogs my only comforters?'   And then,
What meant that strange conclusion : ' If the law
Avail not, nor the prophets, who will hear,
Though one returning from the dead should speak ?
Had we not listened to the law of God,
Who read it day and night?   What need had we
Of new persuasion?   If the thing might be,
That rising from the dead, what more could come
Than what we knew already?   Every bound
Of Heaven and Hell our scribes had mapped and
          planned, .
As men mark out the region of their home,
Assigning that to these, their friends, themselves,
And this to heathens, or Samaria's sons,
Or hated rivals.'
                    "So I reasoned still,
And turned away in anger.   But the dream
Pursued me ; night and day it filled my soul ;
The speechless terrors banished all my rest ;
I panted after peace.   And so I came
Once more to hear, not now with curling lip,
And brow uplifted, but with eager step,
Low bending down, (I, Lazarus, the rich,
The ruler, bowing at His feet who came
From Nazareth, the carpenter !)' I sought
With words of studied honour, on my knees,

To gain the peace I needed. 'What good thing,
O thou good teacher, wilt Thou bid me do,
That I may call the Life Eternal mine?'
I asked in earnest, but it pleased Him not,
That ready homage. 'Why speakest thou of good?
Why comes that word so lightly from thy lips,
When none is good but God? If true thy search
For Life Eternal, keep His holy Laws,
The few great words which in thine earliest years
Thy mother taught thee.' Then, as one who gives
A child his lesson, one by one He spake
The precepts which our Jewish boys repeat,
As of the Second Table. I, amazed,
Looked still for something more. Had I for this
Come, fighting down my pride, to climb the heights
Of truth and wisdom, willing to accept
New rules of fasting, or new forms of prayer,
Or with the Nazarite's vow to cleanse my way?
And now the Teacher sent me back to school,
To take my place there on its lowest form,
With boys of ten? So, not without a touch
Of anger and reproof, I answer made,
' All these are common and familiar things,
And I have kept them from my earliest youth.
What lack I yet to make my life complete?'
Then, with a smile half-sad, as one who sees
In some high-minded, noble boy the germs
Of future evil, so He looked on me

With wistful pity.   And he kissed my brow,
As Rabbis do with scholars whom they love,
And with a subtle tone of something more
Than met the ear, went on.   'Ah ! this is well ;
But yet thou lackest one thing.   Sell thy goods,
Give to the poor, and, taking up thy cross,
Follow thou me, and thou, be sure, shalt have
Treasure in Heaven.'

        " I heard, dismayed and sad,
The words that came like lightning o'er my soul,
And blasted all my hopes.   To give up all,
The silver, and the garments, and the lands,
And be as those who by the Temple-gates
Sit asking alms ;—would nothing less suffice,
No copious tithes of corn, and wine, and oil,
Extending to the cummin and the mint ;
No bounteous offerings to the Corban chest,
So large that men should spread with trumpet
  voice
My praises through the land ?   I never dreamt
Of such a work as this ; and yet beyond
That depth His words disclosed a lower deep.
Not poverty alone, but shame and woe ;
To bear my cross, as I have sometimes seen
The sad procession pass our city's gates,
Each rebel-robber bearing on his back
The beam on which to hang.   Is this the King,
The Son of David, the expected Christ,

Who comes to give us freedom?   Am I called
To follow Him in that?
                         "I turned aside
With brow o'erclouded, and with downcast eyes
That told of inward conflict, half-impelled
To yield to Him whose words had thrilled my soul,
Half-shrinking from the sacrifice He claimed.
Slowly I turned, and as I went my way,
I heard that clear, calm voice in saddest tones,
'How hardly shall the rich man find out God,
And enter into Heaven!'   And then a sound
Of murmured questions, and, at last, once more,
The same low sweetness, as of one who prays,
'Impossible with man, but not with God;'
And then I heard no more.
                         "Ere many days
A fever laid me low : through all my veins
Rushed the hot blood that filled with spectral forms
The darkness round me.   What availed it then
To count the coin, the garments, and the bonds?
Those golden wine-cups would not quench my thirst;
Those gems showed hideous on my purpled skin ;
The spikenard ointment served no more for feasts,
Breathing its odorous breath : they kept it back
For that last use when o'er the senseless dead,
All stiff and cold, they pour the rich perfume.
So sharp the fever that it smote me down,
Left me no power to think, or will, or pray,

One painful stupor till its course was run ;
And round me came the mourners, wailing loud,
(The best were hired in all Jerusalem,
As suited to my rank) and raised their cries,
' Ah me ! my brother, who will comfort now
Thy sisters and thy friends ?   Ah me !   Ah me !
The God of Abraham takes thee to thy place
In Abraham's bosom,' and with claspèd hands,
Beating their breasts, they went on, hour by hour,
' Alas !   Ah me !   Who now will be our joy ?
Our eyes' desire is taken at a stroke.'
And then the Rabbis gathered, some who came
Because they loved me, some in pride of state,
To show that they too knew me, and they spake
Of all my many virtues : ' What a life
Cut off before its time !   In ten years' space
He might have been, of all our Sanhedrim,
Held most in honour !'—Then, with 'bated breath,
' But after all, what is, perchance, is best.
He had his weakness, half-inclined to own
That half-mad Nazarene.   Those sisters there
Have made no secret of it.   Rumour tells
They had Him to their house.   Well, let us hope
This warning blow may bring them back to us.'
So spake they, but they knew not all the while
I heard them in Gehenna.   In mine ears
Their praise was hateful, and that ' half-inclined '
Came floating to me as the knell of doom,

The witness of my guilt. But 'half-inclined!'
Oh! had that 'half' been whole I had not been
In that thick darkness, wailing bitterly.
How long I lay I knew not, for the lost
Count not their time by days, and months, and
    years,
But one long, dreary, everlasting Now
Is ever with them. Every thought of sin
Becomes a drear abyss of boundless woe,
And every act, a moment's sudden heat,
Expands into an æon. All my life
Lay spread before me as an open scroll;
The earliest lust, the boyish greed of praise,
The false dissemblance, and the speech unkind,
These came upon me from the abysmal depths
Where Memory's fountains pour their seething
    floods,
And whelmed me in their torrent. Ah! my son,
If 'twere for this Jochanan sent thee here,
Heed thou my words. The man who once has
    looked
Behind the veil which severs death from life,
He would not venture, all the world to win,
One single thought against the Eternal Law.
We know not now the power of every soul
To be its own tormentor. Here on earth
We cheat ourselves with comfort. Easy days,
And pleasant feasts, and praise of many friends,

These dull our thoughts.   Amid the din of arms,
Or strife of sects, or words of hot debate,
Or painter's art, or skill of poet's speech,
Or sweetest music, we forget our guilt,
And drug our spirits to a death-like sleep :
With loud-toned prayers, and anthems full and clear,
We drown the inward voice : the scribe, self-blind,
Examining his conscience, shuts out God.
But there no shadows come between the soul
And that consuming holiness of God :
There, face to face, we stand before the Light
That lighteth all men, and its glorious rays,
The joy and bliss of all who love the Truth,
Become, for those who hate, the Eternal Fire :
And Memory dwells not there on former years,
As now, with pleasant thoughts of pleasant sins,
But preying on the spirit evermore,
Lives on and on, the worm that dieth not.

"So was I, hopeless in my utter woe,
When, breaking through the silence of the grave,
Through all the darkness of that drear abyss,
The same clear voice cried, 'Lazarus, come forth ;'
And once again I woke, as from a dream,
Looked out once more upon the world of life,
And swathed in grave-clothes, head and hands ard
        feet,
Stood there all wondering, looking out on Him

Whose word had called me.   Still His cheeks were
    wet
With tears of love, of tenderness, of grief;
The sounds of prayer still trembled on the lips;
The eyes were bright, as when the angels look
With joy from Heaven on one repentant soul.
And then I saw it all, the love, the power,
The wisdom, that had guided all the past.
In that strange story which had roused my fears
No Lazarus came to tell the secret things
That lie behind the veil, but now on earth .
There stood a Lazarus who had looked on death,
And lived to bear his witness.
                     " Need I tell,
My son, the further story of my life?
The change was wrought.   I stayed no longer now;
But bore at once the Cross.   They sought my life;
I lived each day as still expecting death;
And gave up all I had, and fed the poor
In one great feast, to which the Master came,
With all His followers.   Martha showed her love,
Still active, eager, but by love made free
From all her many cares, and Miriam now,
Her joy and gladness rushing into act,
Brought forth her precious ointment, costly store,
That might have paid a labourer all his wage
Throughout the circling year, and poured it out
Upon the Lord's dear feet.   I spake not then;

Upon my lips the seal of silence lay,
And still the fear of death was on my soul.
'Is Hades conquered?' I had asked when first
I looked on light anew, 'or must I die
The common death of all men?' Could I smile,
Hearing I stood, death's terrors still in sight,
As men may smile who have not crossed the stream?
Not so, but thought and vigil, prayer and fast,
These filled the hours, and evermore I sought
To know how He who saved me lived His life,
Not with the crowd, or teaching in the streets,
Or breaking bread with friends, but when alone
He with His Father communed secretly.
And one clear moonlight night I followed Him
To that calm garden of Gethsemane,
Where oft He made resort.   All now was gone,
My land, my gold, my robes ; I kept back nought
But the few weeds I wore, and still I stored,
As precious relic of a priceless boon,
The winding-sheet of linen, white and clean,
In which they wrapt me.   At the midnight hour,
Casting that sheet around me, I stole on,
From Bethany and over Olivet,
And neared the garden.   As the moonlight shone,
I saw the three, the foremost of the Twelve,
Weary and spent with toil, stretched out in sleep,
As men too tired to watch, too weak to pray.
But He was there, the pale face paler seen,

As on it fell the moonbeams, and the sweat
Dropt down from brow and face in agony;
And as I nearer drew, I heard the cry
(Strange echo of the words once heard before),
'With Thee, O Father, all is possible.'
And then, as yielding up His will to God's,
He left it all to that Almighty Love
To give or to refuse.
           " What more I saw
I need not tell.   Thou know'st it in the tale
Which every Church receives, the shame, the scourge,
The cross, the death, the burial, and the morn
Of that bright Rising.   Yet there dwells with me
One moment in my life I may not pass.
As I stood listening, from the Kedron vale
The crowd streamed forth, with torches, clubs, and
       swords,
And thronging through the garden seized on Him,
And led Him captive.   The eight, and then the
       three,
Alarmed, confused, forsook their Lord and fled.
I followed breathless, but the moonlight's gleam,
Falling on that white robe, betrayed my form;
And, seeing in me one they sought to slay,
They seized me also, caught the linen sheet,
And when I left it in their hands and fled,
And plunged into the darkness, there I knelt
(The cold moon falling on the olive boughs

To which I fled for shelter) naked, poor,
Hunted, alone.[7]   'Now,' thought I, 'there is hope;
The world has left me homeless as my Lord;
No single rag of all his former state ·
Now cleaves to Eleazar.'
                         " Since that hour
Full fifty years have passed; yet still I live
As one who asks for this day's bread alone.
I toil, and am content.   Through all the change
Of life I bear my cross, and follow Him :
On distant shores, amid an alien race,
My brethren's foes, I linger out my days.
My sisters did their work, and fell asleep,
And I am left alone ; yet not alone,
For Christ, my Lord, is with me.   Thou, my son,
Hast seen me how I live; and I have told
The tale Jochanan bade thee ask to hear.
And now the stars are shining, and mine eyes
With age and thought are weary : and lest I,
Like those three sleepers in Gethsemane,
Should fail to watch one hour, I bid thee go.
Watch thou and pray ; and if to-morrow's sun
Rise on thy soul with healing on its wings,
Or if there dwells aught yet upon thy soul
Wherein thou seekest counsel, come once more
And open out thine heart; and I will speak,
As Christ has taught me through these circling years,
The secrets of His truth.   His peace be thine !"

So parted they, the old man and the youth :
One turning to his skull, his cross, his book ;
One wandering through the strange bewildering
   town.
And over all the moon poured golden light,
And fair Massilia's waters slumbered calm ;
And fairer yet and calmer were the thoughts
That dawned, faint-gleaming, on the wanderer's soul;
But as the moonlight, flecked and dimmed with
   clouds,
Shone on the waters rippled by the breeze,
So o'er his spirit passed opposing moods,
Now bright with hope, now half perplexed with fear,
Now clear in faith, now clouded o'er in doubt.

April, 1864.

LAZARUS.

II.

THE morning came, and then they met once
    more,
The grey-haired saint, whose second path of life
Was near its end, and he, in youth's full strength,
The wanderer seeking truth, and light, and help.
They both had told their story, and their hearts
Were opened, and as face doth answer face,
So talked they freely, mirroring the thoughts,
Each of the other.   And the younger spake,
" Thy words, my father, dwell within my soul,
Like fire that burns and cleanses.   For myself
The path is clear, the way that leads to God,
Through tears, and dread, and darkness : evermore
To bear within my heart His perfect Law,
His Word that cleaves the secret depths of life ;
To conquer self, renounce the glittering world,
My life being hid with Christ.   And, if alone
I stood, or strove, as those who run their race,
To win my prize, regardless of the res;,

This were enough. But as I walked last eve
Massilia's streets, far other thoughts than these
Came thronging on me. From this holy shade
Wherein thou liv'st I passed to Babel's glare,
Mad songs of riot, words of shameless lust,
Foul misery plunging into fouler mire,
Hard-toiling men, their day of labour done,
Sleeping brute-sleep, to whom no vision comes
Of life full-orbed, or God's o'erstretching Love ;
And, as I looked and thought, the question grew
Distinct and clear, and would not be denied,
Which never till thy word had changed my life
I dreamt of asking. These poor, wandering sheep,
What have they done that they should pass away
To those dark shadows of the drear abyss ?
They do the world's rough work, they delve and
          toil,
None caring for their souls, and pass away
Without one ray of light that falls on us,
Without one hope that looks beyond the grave.
These harlot-girls who flaunt along the streets
With pencilled brows, and filmy, saffron vests,
And warbled song, and winning, wanton dance ;
These boys with gleaming eyes and golden hair,
Their waving locks all wet with odorous nard,
Who, knowing not the baseness, stain their youth :
These Gauls and Thracians, torn from distant shores,
Herding, like brutes, by hundreds in their dens,

Butchered when Rome makes merry, — all the
　　crowds
'That throng the marts, the ships, the camps of men,
What future lies before them?   Must I think
That one great torrent sweeps them on to Hell,
That they who never heard the name of God,
Nor knew His righteous will, shall first awake
To that clear knowledge in the hopeless fires?
I look around, and here and there I see
One lonely soul who struggles after truth :
But, far and wide, the thousands live and die,
Unknowing of the greatness of their lives ;
And when I travel o'er the tracts of space,
Or look behind me on the expanse of time,
The same drear vision meets me.   And I ask,
' Can this be all that Christ has come to win?
Is this the bruising of the serpent's head?
Is this the triumph of the victor's car?
Sees He in this the travail of His soul,
And with it rests content?'   I spake but now
Of men and women who have lived their lives ;
But what of all the myriad souls that pass
Their few short hours on earth, and then are gone?
That child of harlot-mother, born in sin
And left to perish ;—has God's gift of life
For those few pain-fraught moments brought on it
The woe that runs through all the endless years?
Or if you tell me that His Love is wide,

That infants whom His Church receives are saved,
Cleansed by the healing waters, then I ask,
Can all the future age of woe or weal
Turn on that chance which they nor know nor care
To ask for, or refuse? Or if, once more,
You tell me of a Love diviner still,
Embracing all, baptized or infidel,
To whom death comes as infant's gentle sleep,
Then subtle questioning brings the doubt again ;
' If they are safe within the arms of God,
Through all the eternal ages, sure to fail,
If childhood's life pass on to conscious will,
Why should not then a mother's tenderest love,
Stifling her nature's instinct, crush the life
That from her draws its nurture, prizing more
That endless bliss than all the smiles and tears,
The waxen touches and the clinging grasp,
Which joy a mother's heart? If this be true,
Our hearts should leap for joy and give God thanks,
When harlots slay the issue of their shame,
When nations, sunk in darkness, cast their babes
A prey to dogs and vultures, when the plague
Sweeps o'er the earth and lays its thousands low,
Or earth's deep fires burst forth from inward depths,
And pour their boiling torrents, as of late,
On fair Pompeii down Vesevus' slope,[1]
Enshrouding in that tomb of burning dust
The mothers and their children.' Woe is me !

D

I tremble, oh, my father ! as I speak
The thoughts that haunt me.   In thine eyes, per-
    chance,
They seem too bold.   They trespass on the ground
Where men must walk in darkness.   But to thee
I open all my heart, for thou hast seen
What others have not.   Thou canst meet my
    doubts,
And tell me of Gehenna ; thou must know
The armies of the lost, and of the saved ;
And therefore blame me not, if I, in words
All rough and hasty, bring those doubts to thee."

   He ceased ; and then the old man looked on
    him,
Not with uplifted hands, and brow that told
Of holy horror, but with wistful thought,
Admiring, pitying, loving.   And he spake :
" Fear not, my son, to tell me all thy soul ;
Thy doubt outspoken may perchance pass on
To purer faith.   The fault that saps the life
Is doubt half-crushed, half-veiled ; the lip-assent
Which finds no echo in the heart of hearts ;
The secret lie, which, conscious of its guilt,
Atones for falsehood by intenser zeal.
These questionings of thine, I know them all,
Know too they come but as the signs of life :
Our Rabbis heed them not : they read and pray,

Debating in their synagogues and schools,
Detecting this man's faults, and grudging that
The honour he has earned.   They little care
What happens to the crowd.   They look with scorn
Upon that crowd, 'the people of the earth';
Filling high places at the feasts of men,
They count on higher at the feast of God,
And that suffices.   But from thee, my son,
Far be that poor content: speak out thy thought
As Abraham spake it, when he asked of God,
'Shall not the Judge of all the earth do right?'
As Job, when, smarting in his sore distress,
He claimed acquittal.   I condemn thee not:
And yet, my son, I cannot grant thy prayer;
I cannot solve the problems of thy soul.
In those few days I passed beyond the veil.
I learnt to know myself, to fear and love
The Lord my Maker; but that lore sufficed;
I could not rise to yon supernal height
Whence all the wonder of the world is seen,
And all the ages in their ordered plan.
That secret dawns not on the new-born life;
The mystery of God remains uncleared;
Into these things the angels seek to look,
Yet see not far.   Let others dream their dreams,
Map out the world of Hades, mark the lines,
As though they knew the country, I, for one,
Must own I know it not, and if I speak

As one whose eyes are opened, know, the Light
Shines on me from within.   No fearful forms
Of spectral horrors float before mine eyes,
But Christ, my Lord, has led me on to truth;
His Spirit quickens all my power to see.
And yet, my son, it may be that thou ask'st
Not wisely of this matter.   I have known,
Ere now, that craving.   Many eyes have looked
Across the abyss, and many lips have asked,
With varying accents, 'Are the saved ones few?'
Some seek that knowledge in their pride of heart,
As finding greater glory in the thought
Of crowds beneath them, failing where they win;
And some in selfish fear lest place should fail
For them in heaven; and some, my son, like
          thee,
In wistful love and pity.   But to none
Is the full answer given : and, evermore,
The veil, uplifted for a moment's space,
Falls once again, and hides the rest from view.
So was it once when Christ our Master taught,
And one came eager, asking as thou ask'st,
And answer found : 'Strive thou to enter in,
For strait the gate and narrow is the way
That lead to life.'   So was it once again,
When Cephas, asking of Jochanan's fate,
Received his answer, 'What is that to thee?'
He bids us walk by faith and not by sight;

He bids us trust His all-embracing love,
His Father's righteous purpose.
     "Yet He taught
Enough to put to shame our narrowing hearts,
And quicken wider hopes. From out the Book,
Where Scribes and Rabbis find abounding proof
That they alone may call the Lord their God,
He read the tokens of a love that streams
On Jew and Gentile, over bad and good,
As shines the sun in heaven. And thence He told
Of outcasts who had sought the light of God,
Of heathens, whom Jehovah owned as His;
The Syrian leper, cleansed in Jordan's flood,
Sarepta's widow, with her cruse of oil,
The men of Nimrod's city, crouching low
In dust and ashes at the prophet's word,
The queen who, coming from the furthest south,
Communed with David's son of all the thoughts,
Deep, wide, and wondrous, that had stirred her
   heart :
And thus, through all His life He gave us proof,
While working still by self-imposèd law
Within a narrower limit, that His heart
Went forth to all. He shrank not from the touch
Of harlot's hands, or flood of harlot's tears ;
He turned not back when that adulterous wife
At Jacob's well spoke with him,—went and dwelt
For two whole days within Samaria's gates ;

And when that outcast of a cursed race
Knelt to Him in her woe, and found at first
Reluctance, silence, sternness, yet the change
Came soon ; His eye had read her secret soul,
And all she asked He gave.   The soldier rough,
Trained in Rome's legions to a life of war,
Was owned by Him as having nobler faith
Than we of Israel.   Yea, the words went forth :
'From east and west, from north and south, shall
    come
Thousands, and tens of thousands, sitting down
With Abraham, Isaac, Jacob, at the feast
Of God's great kingdom.'   Bolder, stranger still,
He drew two pictures of that last great day :
On one side stood the greatest of our Scribes,
Honoured and trusted, rigorous in their fasts,
Punctual in prayers, paying tithes of all ;
And, on the other, those whose names we loathe,
The dwellers of the Cities of the Vale,
The men of Tyre and Sidon, sunk, as they,
In pride, and lust, and baseness.   'And for these,'
So ran the words, ' shall be the lighter doom,
The fewer stripes, the easier pain and loss ;
For those, the outer darkness, and the wail
Of sharpest woe.'   And then, my son, He told
What oft has given me comfort when dark thoughts
Like those thou speak'st of, haunt and vex my soul,
Words which lift up one corner of the veil,

And show hope's brighter vision ; 'lighter doom' ;
So spake He ; 'for had they too seen my works,
And heard my words, in sackcloth and in dust
Long since they had repented.'   Wondrous words !
Which none might speak but He, the Judge of all,
Who reads the inner depths of each man's heart,
And calls the things that are not into life,
Counting as though they were.   He sees the gleams
Of better thoughts across the murkiest gloom,
The seeds of good amid the howling wastes,
And perfects them at last ; and, in the depths
Of His divine forbearance, suffereth long,   ·
And passeth by transgression.   Those who wait
To meet the bridegroom, they must trim their lamps,
And seek the oil from heaven ; and those who own
Him Master, and from Him their gifts receive,
Must bring their talents —ten, or five, or one—
With usury to their Lord.   But that vast throng,
The multitude of peoples, nations, tongues,
Shall stand before His throne, and every act
Of human kindness He will own as His,
And crown as service rendered unto Him.
Oh ! doubt not, then, my son, but fight thy way
In clearer faith against bewildering fears :
Believe that He who in His pitying love
Embraced the children, not of saintly sires,
Or wise, or mighty, but the low-born babes
Of peasant mothers, whom the cleansing flood

Of baptism never reached, and laid His hands,
Mighty to bless, upon their infant heads;
Doubt not that He looks on, embracing still
All new-born souls that taste the breath of life.
That child of harlot-mother, in His sight
Who judges all, is precious as the babe
Which slumbers peaceful in the enfolding arms
Of saintliest matron. Nor do years alone
Determine childhood. Those who live and die,
Children in knowledge, ignorant, and blind,
Children in spirit, simple, kind, and true,
Children in temper, wayward, changeful, weak,
These too He pities, these He seeks to bless;
Their angels stand as highest near the throne.
So evermore His sentence overturns
Our feebler judgment. Outcasts, whom thou spurn'st,
Shall stand before their God arrayed in white,
And sing for joy, the last become the first;
And Rabbis, saints, and teachers, if they hope
For pardon and for peace, must take their place
Low down with shame, the first become the last.
So in the end the eternal Love will shine;
So at the last the mists and clouds will clear:
Till then from out the cloud there comes the voice
Which speaks in trumpet-tones through every land:
'O house of Israel! O thou church of God!
O parties, sects, disputers! own ye not
Your ways unequal, Mine all just and true?'"

Yet once again, half-shamed to speak again,
Pausing as one who, having asked for help,
And gained it, fears, though wanting more, to ask,
The seeker uttered all his deep desire.
"Thy words give comfort, Father : I can look
With less despair on those poor heathen souls
That throng around me. I can now believe,
As my dear master taught me, that the death
Of Christ our Lord availed for all the world
To purchase peace and pardon. I can feel
One common bond of brotherhood with all :
They too are ransomed, and the Light that shines
On us illumines them. And yet there floats
(Bear with me, Father, if I speak it out)
A vague, dim doubt around me. Deem not, ther.,
My thoughts too bold or subtle ; but there comes
This question, and I cannot find reply :—
' If this be so, if all alike shall stand
On equal ground before the great white throne,
If heathen outcasts gain eternal life,
By law unwritten, or by deeds of love,
What needs this message of the Cross of Christ?
Why leave we not the heathen as they are,
Sure that they too will reach the goal at last?
Why go our teachers forth from land to land,
Braving all terrors of the shore, or deep,
To call those wandering, shipwrecked souls to God;
When, as it seems, they spend their strength in vain,

And add no jot to all their chance of bliss?'
And yet once more: the souls that stand con-
    demned,
Or by the Word revealed, or Law unwrit,
Yet graven in their hearts, what fate is theirs?
Are they for ever doomed to penal fires?
Does God delight to torture? Can it be
His love abates when sudden stroke of death
Cuts off the soul whom that forbearing Love
Was leading to repentance? Here on earth
The will is plastic: stained with many a crime
It yet can struggle upward, and renew
Its vigour like the eagle's. Dare we say
That freedom ends with death? Has God's decree
For ever fixed the casual mood of soul
Of that last moment? Does His will condemn
To endless sin? Or welcomes He, at last,
When sin no longer reigns, the wandering soul
That wakes through death to life? Oh, glorious
    thought,
That wraps the future with a golden dawn,
Where old familiar words and new-born hopes
Seem melting into one! 'The Son of God,
Destroys the works of Sin, the power of Death;'
'Great was the trespass, greater still the love.'
'A time shall come when all shall pass away,
All foes o'ercome, and guilt and darkness gone,
And God be all in all, the eternal Love

Prevailing, conquering, binding men to God.'
Ah me! my Father; now I dream my dream
Of one broad, mighty, everlasting peace,
The concord of a universe at rest;
And now once more the mists and shadows come
Between my soul and God, and fear shuts out
That full assurèd hope, and sterner words
Come back unbidden, shattering all my joy.
Broad were the lines He traced, the Lord of Love,
The sheep and goats, the lost ones and the saved;
And evermore, when speaking of the doom
Of that great day, He spake of endless woe,
The quenchless fire, the worm that cannot die,
The punishment which with the life must be
Co-equal, co-eternal. And yet,—and yet;
(Oh! pardon thou these wandering thoughts of
        mine)
New words recur of hope. One only sin,
So spake He, neither in the world that is,
Nor in the world that comes, can ever gain
Forgiveness. Only of the traitor's soul
Were the words spoken, 'It were good for him
That he had ne'er been born.' I ask myself,
Might not that doom, if former fears were true,
Be written on the universe of God,
On all the countless myriads that have passed
In darkness to the grave? If thou canst solve
These riddles, O my Father! if thy soul

Has gone beyond the doubts that come and go,
Unfold the secret.   One has told, I know,
Of torments lasting their appointed time,[2]
Of fires that, burning, cleanse the sin-stained soul,
Of cycles strange through which our spirits pass,
Tasting new forms of life, or man or brute,
Tested and tried till they too rise to God,
And in the fields Elysian find their rest,
Or lose their separate being, to the All
Returning once again.   But these, perchance,
Are but a poet's fancies.   Thou canst guide
My tottering feet through these bewildering mists
In which I wander, wavering and perplexed,
Staggering like drunken man in fevered dreams."

Then Eleazar spake.   "Ah me ! my son,
Thy questions come as fast and wild as winds
Of autumn ; and they vex thee, as the blasts
Vex the deep waters of a mountain lake.
Here once again I bid thee walk by faith :
Nor I, nor thou, can see the mystery clear.
But wonder not, if thoughts should lead thee on,
Each starting from divinest, wisest words,
To issues which agree not.   Evermore
We see the sides of truth, and cannot grasp,
So low we stand, the greatness of the whole.
Thus God elects, yet man is free to choose ;
And God, foreseeing evil, lets it be,

Yet evil is not His; and Christ our Lord,
One with the Father in His boundless might,
Is one with us in all that makes us weak;
And God hath shown His Love in sending Christ,
Yet Christ by death hath reconciled to God
The creatures else condemned; and God is One,
Yet evermore we praise the threefold Name,
The Father, and the Spirit, and the Son.
So fares it with all mysteries of God;
Men cannot bring them to the rule and line
Of earthly wisdom, or with subtle art
Build up their systems.   Broad, o'erarching all,
They float above us, and with hopes or fears
We watch their changing aspects.   And we need
Both hopes and fears: we may not cast aside
One truth that Christ has spoken, may not say
To all the heedless souls that turn from God,
'Go on, and sin; the end is still the same,
The journey only longer;'—dare not close
The door of hope which Christ Himself throws
          wide,
Nor lose from sight the many stripes, and few,
The lighter, heavier woes.   Our feebler thoughts
Dwell on the outward symbols of the doom,
The worm, the fire, the darkness, and the scourge.
But thou, my son, hast learnt the doom itself.
These are but signs and figures of the true,
Shadows of things that are.   The enduring pain

Is memory of evil seen at last
As evil, hateful, loathsome. Pleasant sins,
Which here the doer of the wrong recalls
With faint vibrations of the former sense,
There evermore are present to the soul
In all their foulness, and we feel the wrath
Eternal then unveiled. And hence the woe
Is endless : there we cannot drug our souls,
Or blot from sight the ever hateful past,
The feignèd semblance, or the open shame.
We cannot change that past ; through all the years
Its woe is with us, shading all the life
In gloom of twilight, or in thickest night
Deepening the blackness. To the souls that sinned
In ignorance of God, His grace may come
In mercy wide and free, revealing Light
To those in darkness, blotting out the guilt
Of sins of wild confusion, leaving still,
Through endless æons, all the inward pain
Which waits on conscious sin. To cancel that
Were to undo the eternal work of God,
And leave them still in blindness. And to dream,
As some have dreamt, of agony of sense,
The burning flame, and thick-ribbed ice in turn,
As having power to purify and cleanse,
As greater terrors than the accusing thoughts,
The voice that speaks in thunder, and the wrath
Eternal of the All-knowing and All-good,

This is to take the shadow for the truth,
And live in outward symbols.   Golden throne,
Bright gates of pearl, and walls of amethyst,
The pure clear river, and the mystic tree,—
These are but tokens of the inward bliss,
The vision of our God, to pure hearts given
As life, and peace, and joy.   And so the woe,
Which makes the doom of evil, is to see
That face averted. . God, whose Name is Love,
Condemns the unloving : so we see in Him
That Light eternal, that consuming Fire ;
And still the question meets us as of old,
'What child of man can face that ceaseless flame,
And dwell with burnings everlastingly ?'
And evermore, as once from Prophet's lips,
The strange, bold answer reaches unto us,
'He who the truth hath spoken, right hath done,
Who, fearing God, has conquered self and sin,
He need not fear the fire.'   It burns and burns,
Consuming what is worthless, cleansing still
The pure, bright gold, the treasure of our God.
    "And if these thoughts still leave a darkened space
Through which no light can pierce, if awful words
Speak of persistent evil, wills that, fixed
In hate, defiance, scorn, reject the Light,
Increasing through the endless age their woe,
As adding still fresh deeds of deeper guilt,—
Who then am I to question and to judge?

I bow before the judgment, and am dumb;
I cannot tell how evil first began,
Or why through all the mystery of the world
It runs its course, and all creation groans
In bondage, panting, struggling to be free.
I cannot tell if it shall cease to be,
Or when or how, the final victory won,
The conquering Christ shall yield his throne to
    God;
Or if the conquest shall destroy the works
Of sin and death, or leave them as they are,
His curse upon them. All I know is this,
That God is holy, and that righteous wrath
Must fall for ever on the soul that sins;
That God is Love, and willeth not the death,
Or here, or there, of any soul of man.
And if I see not how, in secret depths,
(The light and darkness melting into one)
The discords of the world are harmonised,
The truths that clash brought once again to peace,
I find my stay in old, familiar words,
The key-note of my life, and all its thoughts,
True of that life through all its wondrous course,
True of the world through all its circling years,
True of the endless ages as they pass,—
Words that rebuke the doubter, bow our pride,
Refresh the mourner, strengthen all our prayers,
The words for thee, my son, when vexing thoughts

Distract thy soul, and fill thy heart with fears;
Make answer thou, with firm unwavering faith,
Against those doubts, as Christ made answer once,
'Impossible with man, but not with God.'
   " For thee, at least, the path is clearly traced :
Do thou thy Master's bidding.   If He came,
Enduring all the torture and the death,
To speak to all men of His Father's love,
Thou, too, if thou hast learnt to think His thoughts,
Must speak to them of Him.   Thou may'st not
      leave
Those souls to wander in their hopeless night,
Nor make the mercy of thy God a cloak
For coward sloth, nor, rapt in visions high,
Forget the present.   If thou see'st the wrong,
Rebuke it; if the many sin and die,
In pity to their souls, hold not thy peace,
But warn them of the Everlasting Fire,
And win them with the Everlasting Love.
And oh ! my son, beware lest pride of heart,
Or yearning pity, or thy zeal for God,
Lead thee to change His order.   Not in vain,
Taught He at first, by fear of endless woe,
In parable and drama shadowing forth
The doom of evil.   Men must learn to hate
The accursèd self that keeps their souls from God;
Must learn to feel the burden of their guilt,
As measured by the woe which God assigns

In that dark prison which the Eternal Love
Hath ordered in its wisdom and its might :
And some may find the lesson hard to learn,
And, knowing not thy thoughts, may miss their way,
If thou should'st leave the simple, open path
Which Christ hath trodden. Teach as He hath
        taught,
Not halving truths, in haste of jealous strife,
Nor twisting words awry with subtle art,
Not speaking where the voice of Christ was dumb,
Nor silent where He spake.   Judge thou thyself,
And leave the greater task to greater power ;
Commit thy friends, thy brothers, yea, thy foes,
The myriads, past, and present, and to come,
To Him who sitteth on the Eternal Throne,
The Son of Man, and yet the Lord of All,
The Judge, the Priest, the Saviour, and the Friend.
Thou canst not gauge His drear abyss of wrath,
Thou canst not fathom all His boundless love,
Thou canst not track His footsteps on the deep ;
And still if doubt, or grief, or hope, or fear
Perplex thee for the future or the past,
Cling to His cross for shelter, own thy guilt,
Thy shame, thy blindness, and with veilèd face,
Low in the dust, be silent and adore."

May, 1864.

THOUGHTS OF A GALATIAN CONVERT.

A.D. 57.

———◦◦———

THESE are strange times; I stand as half-
    perplexed
Which way to turn amid the war of creeds :
New names are heard among us—Moses, Christ ;
Our fathers knew them not, and yet the suns
Rose brightly on them, and the glad showers fell,
And life was pleasant on the vine-clad hills.
They loved and were beloved; they toiled and
    died.
Why has this change come o'er us ? Why disturb
The good old order of the earlier days ?
Why should this flood of vexing questions come,
Disturbing all our peace, and making life
One weary struggle after distant joy,
One painful journey through a trackless waste ?
    And yet the world was evil. This I know,
Though I have seen but little : I have heard
In distant Attaleia, by the sea,

Of those great cities of the western world
Corinth the rich, and Rome magnificent,
And Athens, home of Wisdom ; and the tales
Men told me made me shudder.   Lust and greed,
Envy and hate, and all things rank and vile,
Grew rampant in their baseness.   None were true,
None brave or pure ; before an emperor's throne,
Adoring as a god the tyrant lord,
Baser than all his slaves, men bowed their heads
In self-debasing homage.   Truth was crushed ;
And those who might have helped her silent stood,
Or, wrapt in idle musings, reasoned much
Of destiny, and happiness, and chance,
(None wiser for their talk), perplexing more
The tangled problems of this life of ours.
    We, too, have seen in our Galatian fields
What that great world was like.   To these our hills
Prætors have come to snatch from toil-worn hands
Their scanty earnings, and the locust brood
Of those fierce legions ravaged all our vales.
We dared not murmur : we could only bear
Our ills in silence, or at best might bribe
The shameless ruler, glad enough to keep
The little that he left us, shuddering still
As the proud Roman's wandering glance surveyed
The goodliest and the noblest of our youth,
Our sons and daughters, picking out his slaves,
That they, too, might be vile, and eat the bread

Of loathsome bondage.   Yes, the world went wrong ;
Hope's dreams had faded ; what the poets sang
Of great Augustus was belied by time.
No golden age had come : the old disease
Was still unhealed, the old crimes re-appeared.
A change was needed ; yet the skies were dark,
And no bright streaks of dawn were in the East ;
The oracles were silent, and the gods
Seemed waxing feeble ; and our faith grew weak,
According to their weakness.   Hymns of praise
Were but an idle rending of the air ;
And as for prayers—who dreamt the gods would
        hear ?
Who feared their vengeance ?   Could we hope that
        they
Would rouse the world from its decrepit age,
And make it young again ?   And so decay
Went on to rottenness ; and mists of doubt
Hung over all our souls, as o'er a fen
The dank fog clings, and poisons while it chills ;
And when we asked the question, "What is truth ?"
No voice made answer from the eternal depths.

And yet among our people, on the heights
Of Phrygia's hills, and round the ancient shrines
Of old Galatian towns, there lingered still
Some traces of the wild, mysterious power,
The spell that bound our fathers to their faith.

The beardless priests of Cybele would wave
Their wands, and clash their cymbals,' and their
    song,
First stealing through the brain with subtle power,
Waking each nerve to tension,—then with floods
Of surging sound tumultuous, sweeping on,
Like some great river foaming in its pride,
Filled all the soul with madness; and the charm,
In one wild, dizzy, whirling, frenzied dance,
Drew all who worshipped; and the drops poured
    down
From pallid brows and languid limbs, till night
Fell on them with its darkness, covering deeds
Yet darker; and the morning grey looked in
On haggard faces, spectral forms, and eyes
Ghastly and vacant, drunk, but not with wine.
I, too, have known all this, have felt the blood
Rush like a boiling torrent through my veins,
Half-tempted, in the madness of the hour,
To be as Atys was, and like her priests
To serve the Goddess-mother; but the sense
Of memory, waking in me, held me back,
The hopes of many summers, and the face
Of one fair, bright-eyed maiden on the hills.

    So life went on. Near thirty years had passed,
When through our village came the strangest band
That ever travelled through Galatia's vales:

No merchants they, with pearls, or purple robes,
Or precious spikenard in the milk-white vase,
Or golden goblets ; no centurions, come
To take our numbers, and to tax our farms ;
Nor yet as pilgrims hasting to the shrine
Of Pessinus, where Cybele holds sway,
Mother of all the gods, with crown of towers.
Like none of these they came, those travellers
    three ;
One in full age, dark-eyed, with eagle face,
Like those whom in Pisidian synagogues
Men know as Rabbis.   Grave he was, and oft
Could speak to touch men's hearts, and stir their
    fears
With words of coming woe : yet not of him
Thought we most then, or most remember now.
The next was young and slender, scarcely past
His eighteenth summer, gentle as a girl,
Shrinking from each rude gaze, or jesting word ;
A hidden fire within his lustrous eyes,
Telling of musings deep ; and pale, thin cheeks,
Bearing their witness of the midnight watch
And fast prolonged, and conquest over self ;
Timotheos, so they called him, won our love,
And paid it back with tears : yet not of him
Thought we most then, or most remember now.
The third who journeyed with them, weak and
    worn,

Blear-eyed, dim-visioned, bent and bowed with pain,
We looked upon with wonder.   Not for him
The praise of form heroic, supple limbs,
The glory of the sculptor as he moulds
The locks of Zeus o'erspreading lofty brows ;
Apollo, the Far-darter, in the pride
Of manhood's noblest beauty, or the grace
Of sandalled Hermes, messenger of gods :
Not thus he came, but clad in raiment worn,
Of roughest texture, bearing many stains
Of age and travel.   In his hand he bore
A staff, on which he leant as one whose limbs
Have lost before their time the strength of youth ;
And underneath his arm a strange, old book,
Whose mystic letters seemed for him the words
Of wisdom and of truth.   And oft he read,
In solemn cadence, words that thrilled his soul,
And, lighting that worn face with new-born gleam,
Bade him go on rejoicing.
                                          So they came ;
So entered he our town ; but, ere the sun
Had lit the Eastern clouds, a fever's chill
Fell on him ; parchèd thirst, and darting throbs
Of keenest anguish racked those weary limbs ;
His brow seemed circled with a crown of pain ;
And oft, pale, breathless, as if life had fled,
He looked like one in ecstasy, who sees
What others see not, to whose ears a voice,

Which others hear not, floats from sea or sky :
And broken sounds would murmur from his lips
Of glory wondrous, sights ineffable,
The cry of " Abba, Father," and the notes
Of some strange, solemn chant of other lands.
So stricken, prostrate, pale, the traveller lay,
So stript of all the comeliness of form,
Men might have spurned and loathed him, passing
    on
To lead their brighter life.   And yet we stayed ;
We spurned him not, nor loathed ; through all the
    shrouds
Of poverty and sickness we could see
The hero-soul, the presence as of One
Whom then we knew not.   When the pain was
    sharp,
And furrowed brows betrayed the strife within,
Then was he gentlest.   Even to our slaves
He spake as brothers, winning all their hearts
By that unwonted kindness.   Those who came
To give some casual help, the grape's fresh juice,
Or golden fruit from Pontus, found a spring
Of new-born feeling flooding all their souls ;
The careless, sportive youths, hard-toiling men,
And mothers worn with age and household work,
And children smiling in their infant glee,
Would gather round his couch ; and each and all
Found it their highest blessing but to soothe

One throb of anguish, and (could such things be)
Would fain have offered health, and strength, and
    youth,
Would fain have given their own bright, gleaming
    eyes,
And walked in darkness, so that he might see.

And then, as strength returned, he spake to us
As none e'er spake before : " I find you friends ;
God's law of love is written on your hearts ;
Ye seek the Unknown, the Lord of Earth and
    Heaven,
The Father of us all.   And yet I see
In every home the forms of household gods ;
Ye bow before dumb idols.   Vain deceit,
Transmitted from your fathers, wraps you round ;
Ye know not that the Lord your God is One,
Not far off, dwelling on Olympian hills,
Beyond the furthest Ocean's western glow,
Or down in shadowy realms of Hades dark,
But near, around, within you.   Turn, oh ! turn
To Him who seeks you, calls you.   He has spread
Through all the world the tokens of His love,
The showers from Heaven, and fruitful years, and
    joy
Of vintage and of harvest.   In the soul
Of man himself He wakens solemn dread,
And questionings that stir the depths of life,

And yearnings after peace, the sense of guilt,
Vague hopes and vaguer fears. Yet men are blind,
Blind the untaught, and blinder still the wise,
By wisdom missing God. But through the world
His purpose runs ; and when the time had come,
And Jew and Greek had learnt the bitter truth
That sin and death enslaved them, then He sent,
Born in our flesh, in nature one with us,
His Son, His well-beloved, to set us free."
    Then told he of the works of One who lived
In Galilee, a Prophet, yea, and more
Than prophet e'er had been, for grace and truth
Illumined all His life. He came to heal
Each ill of suffering men, to loose the chains
Of custom, and to bid the oppressed be free,
To tell them of a Father's love, and bind
Their tyrant and destroyer. So He worked
For three short years. And then against Him rose
His nation's priests and rulers, cutting short
The life that shamed them. On the cursèd tree
He died, as die the robber and the slave.
They knew not what they did: the blood that
        streamed
From those blest wounds was like a God's, and
        Love
Was mighty in that death to ransom all,
The countless generations of the past,
Those who now walk the earth, and all to come,

Through circling ages.   Death, and then the grave,
Came as they come to all; but not for Him
The drear abyss of Hades.   Over Him
Death could claim no dominion.   In His might,
As Son of God He rose; as Son of Man
Ascended up on high, and liveth there,
A Priest, a Friend, hereafter Lord and Judge.
  "He claims you as His own;" so ran the words
Of that strange preacher when his tale was done;
" In Him you may find pardon, as even I
Have found it for my trespass, darker far
Than you have ever known; for I blasphemed
That holy Name; I bound, and scourged, and
      stoned
The saints who owned Him Lord: and yet He
      turned
On me His pitying look.   In vision strange,
Within me and without, He met my soul,
And showed me to myself, and bade me know
The glory of His cross.   And now I go,
Bearing that cross through all the lands of earth,
And bidding all the nations turn and look
On Him the Crucified.   He died for you ;
For you He rose again ; for you He lives,
And pleads for you before His Father's throne.
Easy His yoke, His burden light.   To love,
Repent, believe, is all He asks of you :
His simplest gifts in nature come as signs

And pledges of His love.   The running stream
That purifies the flesh shall cleanse the soul ;
The daily bread, the wine that glads the heart,
Are by His great command the flesh, the blood,
He gives to be our life ; the pledges true
Of fellowship with God's great charity."

We listened.   Some still doubted ; others mocked,
As though a dreamer spake, with idle tales
Lulling men's minds to slumber.   I for one,
And others with me, felt that God had sent
His messenger, that these glad tidings came
To call us to His kingdom ; and we owned
The Christ of whom he told us.   Then the two,
Silvanus and Timotheos, led us down
To where the river, in its winding curves,
Leaves a smooth-margined bay.   With trembling
        sense
Of some great change impending, we drew near ;
Naked we stood for that our second birth
As at our first, in spirit putting off
The flesh-stained garments of our sinful youth :
Then entered we the waters ; "IN THE NAME,
THRICE-BLESSÈD, OF THE FATHER, AND THE SON,
AND OF THE HOLY SPIRIT" (so they spake
The mystic words), and o'er us closed the stream,
As the grave closes, and we rose again,
(As Christ, our Master, on that Easter morn),

New-born, new creatures, chosen, heirs of God.
The names were lofty, yet they spake them out,
As doubting nothing, and though memory fails
And thoughts of that high hour are grown confused
With the world's wear, and all the earth-born cares
That since have vexed our souls, I, too, believe
I felt that moment stirrings of a life
Till then unknown, the purpose fixed and strong,
(As when a soldier joins a noble band
Of warriors true) with Christ to live and die,
My Lord, my Leader, yea, my King, my God.

'Twas done, and in the newness of that life
Some few days glided by. We lived alone,
In silent thought retracing all the past;
And then we met once more. At eventide,
When the Jews' Sabbath drew towards its close
(So heard we from our teachers, for no word
Bade us to keep that Sabbath),[2] all the West
Yet purple, we, the new disciples, met
That pale, worn teacher in the upper room,
His home for those few days. A simple meal
Was set before us, cakes of bread, and wine,
Such as our peasants drink. That bread he blest,
Over that cup gave thanks, and we partook,
(The new-born sense of kindred breaking down
All barriers of the past) the rich, the poor,
The slave, the freeman, foes of many years,

Husbands and wives, the fathers, and the sons,
We all drew near, as sharers in a life
Above our own, and so embracing all.
Oh, happiest hour, of memories full of peace,
And love ineffable, and brightest hopes,
Which even yet can gladden !
                               Yet there came
A moment higher still.   Upon our heads
Those feeble hands were laid, and through our
      frames,
With strange vibrations of a rushing flood
Of thoughts and powers fresh kindling into life,
THE SPIRIT came upon us.   From our lips
Burst the strange, mystic speech of other lands,
We, too, cried, "Abba ! Lord of Sabaoth !"
We, too, could raise the Hallelujah chant,
And from our feeble tongues, in wondrous tones,
As of the voice of trumpet, loud and long,
The mighty " Maranatha " smote the air.[3]
We knew not all we spake, but evermore
The clear, loud accents thrilled through all the soul ;
We praised, adoring.   Men might count our words
As wild and aimless, yet to us they brought
The joy ecstatic of the eternal choirs,
The hymns of angels at the throne of God.
And others, calmer in their strength of heart,
Received new power to read the thoughts that
      stirred

In each man's breast, to speak with words of fire,
Swift-darting as an arrow to their mark,
To say to this one, " Thou hast sinned, thy deed
Of secret shame is blazoned on thy brow;"
To that, " Fear not; thy hidden tears are known,
Thy yearning after peace; and God, who loves
The contrite heart, has pardoned all thy sins."

He left us, and for years we saw him not,
But for one passing visit of a day.
Our life resumed its calm, the even months
Went on, but purer, brighter than before:
A little band of brothers, so we lived
As in the world, not of it, honouring all,
Yet loving each the other.   Not for us
The idol-feast, the revel, and the song;
But true work duly done, and converse grave
As though the Lord were listening.[4]   And we met
At sunset still in each returning week,
To break that bread of life, that wine to drink,
As He, the Lord commanded.   But the power
Of that first day returned not.   That full burst
Of prophecy was hushed: the wondrous Tongues
In wild, mysterious sweetness came and went,
Each echo weaker as the months passed on,
Until at last they ceased, and we became
Half weary with the sameness of our lives.

And then there came new travellers, grave and stern,
Rabbis, and scribes, and teachers of the law,
Trained at Gamaliel's feet.   Around their robes
That swept the ground, the broad, bright fringe of
blue
Proclaimed their faith, and o'er each arm there
twined
The sacred scrolls, and when they stood and prayed,
O'er brow and face they drew the mystic veil,
As Moses did of old.   They came from far,
They told us, from Jerusalem the blest ;
They, too, were brethren, worshippers of Christ,
And from the high Apostles went they forth,
From Cephas, James, and John, with power to rule
The Churches, and to perfect all that lacked.
    They came among us, asking how we lived,
What Paul had done for us ; and when they heard
Our simple tale, they lifted up their hands,
And tore their garments ; " What, ye fools, and
blind ?
Ye read the Law, and break it ?   Know ye not
That not one tittle of that Law shall fail ;
And dare ye choose, in your o'erweening pride,
Now this, now that, to keep or cast away ;
And, owning Abraham's God, to slight the seal
Of Abraham's faith ?   Hath not His voice declared,
' The soul that is not circumcised shall die ?'
Yet ye remain as aliens, and the laws

Which God proclaimed from Sinai ye despise.
You tell us, ' Paul thus taught.' We know the man,
The apostate dreamer, breaking down the wall
Which God hath built. We sent him forth to teach,
And, when we found him faithless, cast him off.
We know that tottering frame and trembling step,
True sign of wavering counsels, and a voice
That tunes itself according to the time.
He, too, can speak as we do, when he seeks
To please the Jews, his brethren. Know ye not
That young Timotheos ? Him he circumcised
Who bids you trust in faith without the Law ;
And he who boasts of grace and light within,
Who bids you keep no Sabbaths, hold no feasts,—
He came from Corinth to our Temple-courts,
The Nazarite's vow upon his shaven head,
A pilgrim at our feast of Pentecost."

        Their words seemed strong. We knew not what
            to say ;
And some of us were weak, by subtle spell
Bewitched and overcome ; and some held back,
Stedfast, though trembling, to the truth they
            loved,—
These, frowned upon, shut out, as self-condemned ;
Those, courted, favoured, honoured, led about
As proselytes indeed. I took my place
With those who followed Paul. With heavy heart

And thought half-doubting, still I kept my ground.
I saw no fruit that answered to their boasts,
No spirit-stirring power, or peace, or love;
But envy, strife, debate, the gathering clouds,
Forerunners of a storm : in every home
Three against two divided, and the Church
Crumbled and broken by the war of sects.
They could not read our hearts : no searching
    words
Of insight or of pity won their way
To stubborn souls.   They told not of the Cross,
With all its power to bless; but still they spake
Of Moses, and the Sabbath, and the rules
And customs of the elders, joying most
When greetings loud of " Rabbi " met their ears,
And plenteous offerings filled their spacious bags,
And men bowed down in homage as they passed.
    And now there comes this letter. Bold and strong
Are those clear notes of warning.   " Not from man,
Or man's consent, have I this Gospel preached,
And man shall not control me."   Half in love,
And half in pity, pours the tide of thought,
Its currents strangely mingled.   Much mounts up
To heights I cannot reach.   Its subtle art
In part bewilders;—how the Law, of old,
Was given by angels, 'stablished in the hand
Of one who stood half-way 'twixt men and God,
The mediator, Moses, and in this

Must yield the palm to that diviner word
Which God himself in all his oneness spake
To Abraham and his seed, that seed being Christ,
(No Mediator there)⁵, and we in Him,
Sharing his Sonship, recognised as heirs :
How Hagar, wandering in the desert wild,
The bond-slave with her son, had shadowed forth
The rocks of Sinai terrible and dread,
The bondage of Jerusalem that is ;
While Sara, princess-mother of the free,
Claims as her children all the chosen seed,
Heirs of the heavenly city : once again,
How that the Law was as the slave who leads
The wayward boy to school, and keeps in bounds,
Chastising, warning, checking, till at last
The one true Teacher comes, and, heir of all,
The boy starts up to manhood, and is free.
All this I wondered at, as dazed and stunned
By thoughts so strangely new ; but much is plain
That he may run who reads.   He will not yield
One jot to those his foes, and scorn for scorn
With usury repays.   In tenderest words,
Reminding us of all our former love,
He chides us for our folly, bids us know
That they who seek to glory in our flesh,
In cutting that do cut us off from Christ ;
That not through zeal for God, but fear of man,
They build again the poor, weak thoughts of old,

And prove themselves transgressors.   Yea, at last
In bolder speech, with touch of sarcasm rough,
He tells those preachers of a fleshly rite
That he, for his part, wishes they would make
Their work more thorough, holding rank with those
Who serve the Goddess-mother at her shrines ; ⁶
Fit end for those who linger in the past,
The dead, decaying past, and look not on
To all the freedom of the age to come.
   I too will claim that freedom.   Every pulse
Of old affection kindles into life ;
The mists of doubt are scattered ; and the Truth
Shines clearer than before, and every name
Of our old worship, or of Hebrew law,
Yields to the one great Name, no longer strange,
Of Christ the Lord, the Brother of mankind,
Their Saviour and their King.   Lord, hear our
         prayer :
If ever we have bowed before Thy Cross,
If ever we have looked upon Thy wounds,
When Paul's full speech made present once again
What passed on Golgotha, Oh ! grant us, Lord,
With Paul, to claim thy Spirit, yea, to feel
The travail-pangs, till in our soul be formed
The new, diviner man ; and all our life
Pass on, unwavering, to the Eternal Home.

May, 1864.

JESUS BAR-ABBAS.

W ELL! the escape was narrow. Seven long
weeks
I lay expecting death, for Pilate's wrath
Was kindled into frenzy. I had dared,
When that proud tyrant 'gainst the Lord of Hosts
Had raised his banners, and with hands profane
To build his stately tower by Siloam's pool,
Had seized our sacred Corban,'—I had dared,
I say, to head the Zealots in their fight.
They chose me for their leader; found in me,
Robber and outlaw though I be, the man
They needed for their struggle. But the spears
Of Rome's strong legions smote us, and we fled;
And I, with some few others of our band,
Was seized, and marked for death. Do thou,
O Lord!
For this my zeal forgive me all my sins;
And when I die receive me to Thyself
In Abraham's bosom, where the heroes old

Who fought against the Syrian rest in peace.
I need make some atonement. With these hands
I have made women childless, burnt the huts
Of peasants, seized the traveller on his way,
And left him stript and wounded : this I own ;
Yet am I not so base as others are ;
For never have I bowed the knee in prayer
To any heathen god, and still have kept
The creed my Rabbi father taught my youth ; [2]
And ever, when the solemn seasons came,
We went in pilgrim-guise to keep the feast,
And thronged the Temple courts. A double gain
Those journeys brought : we worshipped, and we
    robbed.
The pilgrims coming with their gifts and gold,
From North and South, from furthest East and
    West,
But chiefly the rich proselytes of Rome—
We marked them for our prey. But most we loved
To glut at once our rapine and our hate,
And, laying hold of some centurion proud,
To bind him hand and foot, to seize his gold,
And mocking all his cries, by fear of death
To make him curse his gods, and, bending low,
Proclaim himself a convert. 'Twas a life
Of hair-breadth 'scapes, and ventures strange and
    wild,
Now starved and naked, now with wine and mirth

Filled to our heart's content.   And so we lived,
A band of brothers, not without the ties
Of equal risks and hopes, until that hour
When, as I said, the Roman soldiers seized
Our struggling troop, and we were doomed to death.
There lay I in my dungeon, bound with chains,
And soldiers keeping guard.   No friends might
          come
To give the robber-chief one kindly look,
Or tell him how the world went on without;
And, those rough Romans speaking scarce a word
Of our old Hebrew, little reached my ears
Of what was passing, till the Paschal feast
Drew crowds of pilgrims.   Then I heard the tramp
Of constant feet below my dungeon walls;
And once a shout, the cry of eager boys
And Galilean peasants, and the throng
Of dwellers in our city.   Loud they raised
Their clear Hosannas, blessing One they owned
As Son of David—Israel's longed-for king.
And he passed by me, in that pageant strange,
Not riding in his chariot, or reclined
In stately litter, but as those of old,
Our judges, rode on asses, so did he;
And, as he came, they shouted, and with palms
Fresh cut bestrewed the way.   I heard the cry,
And said within myself, "This will not last;
I have seen many such.   Rome's mighty arm

Will crush these rebel-kings out, one by one;
And he who now rides on, whoe'er he be,
Will die as I shall die.   Who knows?   Perchance
The self-same hour may witness both our deaths."
Then came a silence.   For some nights and days
I nothing heard, but still expecting death,
Lay there in darkness; when at last a voice
Was heard, in foreign accents, at my cell:
"Bar-Abbas, Pilate calls thee."   "Now," I thought,
"My hour is come at last."   I said my creed,—
"Hear, Israel, hear, the Lord thy God is One,"—[s]
In haste, that I might die as Abraham's son,
And claim my place in Eden.   Then I went,
Close following the centurion who had called;
And as I drew toward the opening gate,
The wild, fierce murmur of the people smote
Upon my ears.   I thought I heard my name
Mingled with cries and curses.   Then I stood
Before great Pilate, in his purple robes,
Upon his pavement seated.   And his voice,
As one half-choked with anger, shame, and grief,
Making me wonder, told me, "Thou art free;
The people claim thee: go thy way and live."
So strange it all appeared, I stood amazed,
As one who, waking from a dream, half doubts
Whether he still be sleeping; but ere long
They told me all the story.   "That poor king,"
They said, "had roused the wrath of all our priests,

And all the hostile schools of rival Scribes,
Baffling their art, and laying low their pride,
And speaking still of judgments sharp and swift
As hanging o'er their heads.   Among the Twelve,
His chosen friends and followers, one they found
A traitor; and by night he led them forth
Across the Kedron to Gethsemane,
Just on the slope of Olivet.   All hushed,
The city slept in moonlight.   Every house
Had had its Paschal feast, when that armed band,
With lights and torches, followed on the track
By which the traitor led them.   Then they seized
Their prisoner; and in haste, at dead of night,
They summoned the great Council of our land
And found him guilty.   Then to Pilate's hall
They led him (for they durst not, of themselves,
Pilate being present, put the man to death),
And clamouring loud, with charges swarming thick,
Pressed eager for his life.   But Pilate's heart
Misgave him, and he would not.   Well he knew
Their malice and their envy.   And the hours
Passed on in wavering counsels : now he spake
In secret with the prisoner, half-inclined
To pity one so weak ; now sent him bound
To Herod for his trial; then perplexed
And fearing, thought to win the people's heart
By offering them a prisoner, whom they would,
For freedom on the instant, doubting not

That they would choose the king whose pageant
    proud
A few days since had swept along the streets.
When lo ! wild shouts of frenzy rent the air,
' Not this man, but Bar-Abbas !' So our priests,
Wily and wise, had planned their scheme before,
Knowing the people loved me for my zeal ;
And, seeing in me still a Rabbi's son,
They plotted for their order. So it was,
We stood there in the presence of the crowd,
That Galilean prisoner-king, and I,
Jesus Bar-Abbas,'—I, in pride of strength,
Towering above the people by a head,
As Saul above the hosts of Israel ;
And he, that other Jesus, standing there,
Pale, worn, and crowned with thorns. I, free at last,
The robber and the murderer, shouts of praise
Still ringing in my ears, and he, the just,
(So Pilate owned him, and his silent calm
Bore the same witness), scourged, condemned to die,
Mocks, taunts, revilings adding stings to death.
    At first the crowd received me, bore me on
As in a car of triumph ; then, half wild
With joy and wonder, following where they led,
I joined the crowd that, streaming through the gate,
Passed on to Golgotha. I stood and watched
The three led forth to death. All faint and weak,
And sinking 'neath the burden of his cross,

The prophet-teacher came.   The other two
Were sharers with me in my outlaw life,
With me had plundered, revelled, dwelt in caves ;
Or in the forest-depths of Gilead's hills,
With me had dared defy our Roman lords,
With me were taken prisoners.   Now their hour
Was come, yet still they quailed not.   Hard and
        bold,
They drank the spicèd wine-cup, which benumbs
The nerves of sense, and through the reeling brain
Sends snatches of old songs, forgotten jests,
And mirth that mounts to madness.   So they met
The torture of that hour : no cry of pain
Came from their lips when through the quivering
        flesh
They drove the torturing nails.   With brow com-
        pressed
And look defiant, they endured the shame,
And hanging there, beneath the sultry sun,
Naked and bleeding, speechless bore it all.
And he was speechless too, the third, whose cross
Between them stood, but oh ! how wide the gulf
That lay between his silence, meek and calm,
Eyes lifted up to Heaven, and murmured prayer,
When those rough soldiers nailed them to the cross,
' Father, forgive them ' (so I caught the words),
' They know not what they do ; ' and that dumb
        wrath,

The fiercer for repression, which in them
Crushed out all pity. Soon the contrast grew
More wondrous still. A love that conquered pain,
The joy of one who sees his work achieved,
The full compassion going forth to all,
These brightened all the furrows of that face
With glory from the Throne. But they, my friends,
When the first throbs were over, waxing bold,
(That well-drugged wine-draught rushing through
        their veins)
With jest as rough, and laugh as loud and free,
As when of old our comrades met to feast
After the day's marauding, turned on him,
That silent sufferer, with reproach and scoff,
Re-echoing taunts that came from worthier lips,
From priests and scribes who stood in pride of
        place,
Exulting o'er their victim; ' Hail, O king !
Thou Son of David on thy father's throne,'
(So spake they with mock homage) ' prove thy
        strength,
Put forth thy might to vanquish all thy foes ;
If thou be Christ, Anointed of the Lord,
Come down unbleeding from the accursèd tree,
And claim us as thine own.' I could not join
Those mockers in their taunts. ' He fills my place ;'
So thought I with myself. ' He dies for me ;
And but for Him I too were hanging there,

My sins upon my head.   From me at least
He claims some pity.'   So I silent stood :
But those, the other two, upon their trees,
Caught up the scoff, and with the keener zest
That torment gives to outrage, raised the cry,
'O Son of David, Lord of Abraham's seed,
O King of Israel, save thyself and us !'
He heard, but answered not.   One pitying look
He turned to those who mocked, one upward glance
Of love and prayer unspoken, and there fell
On him and them a silence.   O'er the sky
A darkness stole, as when the sun's eclipse
Affrights the nations, and the mocks were hushed,
Till yet once more, as if to cheat his pain,
From one poor sufferer came the words of scorn,
'Thou Son of David, save thyself and us !'
But now a change had come.   No echoing voice
Spake from that other cross.   In days of old,
I well remember, Dysmas had a touch
Of woman's softness in him, shrank from blood
Save when the fight was hot, and sometimes turned
To help the stript and plundered as they lay.
I call to mind some thirty summers back,
When first he came among us, brave and tall,
Half-joying in our freedom, half-afraid
Of our wild, lawless life, there came our way
A mother and her child, and one who seemed
To both a fostering father.   Poor they were,

But that we heeded not; unarmed and weak;
That only drew us on.   If small the prize,
Small, too, the danger.   So we seized the three,
And soon had robbed them of their scanty all;
But Dysmas, then some eighteen winters old,
Begged hard for mercy.[5]   Something touched his
     heart;
The mother's grief, that spake to him of home,
The blameless child that smiling stretched his hand,
As pardoning those who wronged him; and he
     asked
One favour only, giving up his share
That day of all our plunder, that the three,
The husband, and the mother, and the child,
By his right hand defended from all foes,
Might journey to the city where they dwelt.
So was it then : and such a change of mood
Passed o'er him now.   I know not if he traced
In that pale, weeping mother, bowed with grief,
And faint, as though a sword had pierced her heart,
The grace and beauty that had swayed his soul;
Or if, perchance, that pitying look of love,
That brow all bleeding with the crown of thorns,
Recalled the smiling child, with outstretched hands,
Rejoicing, loving, trusting.   This I know,
That when the taunting words were heard again,
A righteous anger flushing all his frame,
He spake the stern rebuke : 'And fear'st thou not ?

Is this a time for mock and scoff and jest,
When thou, too, standest face to face with death?
We in our guilt, deserving all the shame,
Reaping the harvest sown through many a year,
While he whom thou revilest, righteous, true,
Obedient, gentle, hath done nought amiss.'
Then, turning with a new-born trust, he looked
To that poor sufferer dying on his cross,
As if he were indeed great David's Son,
Anointed of the Lord : 'Remember me,
O Lord, when thou shalt come in glorious pomp
To claim thy kingdom ; Oh, remember me!'
He spake as one whose heart was pouring forth
The fulness of its craving, all its life
Depending on the answer, all its joy
Wrapt up in that one word, its deepest woe
The thought of being forgotten.   Oft of old,
Like others of our band, he had his dreams
Of that great kingdom of the Christ to come,
The armies conquering at their chief's command,
The arrows sharp to drink the foeman's blood,
The chariot sweeping o'er the prostrate ranks,
The kingly throne on Zion's height restored,
Jerusalem once more a pride and joy.
Such dreams, it may be, floated o'er his soul
In that last prayer.   If so, one single word
Dispersed them.   When the answer came, it spake
Of no proud pageant of the pomps of earth,

But gave the promise of a night of peace
After that noon of torture ; cooling streams
After that fevered thirst ; for writhing limbs,
And naked shame, and taunts of mocking crowds,
The land as Eden fair, where gales of balm
O'er soft, green meadows murmur evermore.
' Fear not ; thou shalt be with me ; ' so the words,
Like low, soft music, sounded in mine ears,
' With me, within the Paradise of God.'
I heard it, and before my soul there rose
A vision of the past, when I, a child,
Guiltless as yet, my hands unstained with blood,
Heard from a mother's lips of that blest home,
And God, and His good angels.   And I looked
At Dysmas, and beheld the languid eye
Kindle with hope, the furrowed brow expand,
The closed lips move in blessing.   More and more,
Unless my sight played false, those features grew
Into another's likeness, imaged back
The calmness of that sufferer on His cross :
The hardness and the stains of many years
Dropt off as in a moment, and disclosed
The nobler nature of the new-born man.
'Twas strange ; I could but marvel as I gazed,
And stranger thoughts stirred in me.   Who was this
That, lifted on the cross, had power to draw
The hearts of all men to him ?   Who might tell
The secret of his life ?   Was this the end,

G

This shame and torture, this prevailing love,
This hour of darkness, this triumphant joy?
    As yet these things are hidden from mine eyes;
They lie behind the veil.   But through my soul,
With lightning force, there flashes the new thought
That not for all the wealth of Rome's great lords,
Nor all the state that dazzled Sheba's queen,
Would I against that Holy One stir hand
Or foot, speak word, or in my thoughts
Plan aught of evil.   This I know, that I,
If by a wish I might undo the past,
Would fain live o'er again my term of years,
Win back the vanished past, and, as of old
I clutched the traveller's gold with eager grasp,
Would seize that kingdom, pressing on in haste,
That none might get before me, owning him
As king, content to follow in his path,
Bearing my cross for him, as now for me
He has borne his.   And when my death-time
        comes,
May that all-pitying look be with me still,
Those tones of mercy lull my soul to rest,
That dream of Paradise enwrap me round!
    What followed then I saw not. Gathering thoughts
Made my eyes dim with strange, unwonted tears,
And full of very shame lest priests and scribes,
Soldiers and people, should detect the change,
'The wild Bar-Abbas in a melting mood!'

I crept away, as thick the shadows fell,
And saw and heard no more.   But I will find,
Soon as the Sabbath sun has run his course,
Some who shall tell me all my heart's desire,
Disciples of the Master whom I too
Am fain to follow.   I will ask of them
What drew them to HIM, how they won his love :
And so, perchance, this day shall be to me
As to our fathers was that Paschal feast,
When Israel came from Egypt, leading on
To life and freedom, making all things new."

June, 1864.

GOMER.

" And the Lord said to Hosea, Go, take unto thee a wife of whoredoms. . .
So he went and took Gomer the daughter of Diblaim."—HOSEA i. 2, 3.

OH, sorrow of all sorrows ! death of deaths !
    The springs of blessing poisoned at their
    source !
The shadows falling ere the day is done !
I watch the ghastly ruins of my life,
The shattered columns of a vanished joy,
And through them wanders every beast unclean,
And o'er them sweeps the moaning of the blast ;
And in my woe I travel o'er again
The strange, drear path that leaves me here alone,
Bowed down in shame, dishonoured, reft of all,
And haunted by the memory of past joys.
Far other was I, when in youth's first dawn
I wandered joyous o'er Samaria's hills,
Life's golden hopes before me. I was clean
From all pollution of the sense or soul ;
I never bowed the knee at Moloch's shrine,
Nor joined in dance to queenly Ashtaroth,

Nor with the black-robed company of priests
Sang praise to Baal in Zidonian fanes :
True to my fathers' fame I kept their faith,
And cleaving to the prophets of our land,
The few bright stars that shone in murkiest night,
Became as one of them.   We lived in peace
Where Jordan's windings glad the palm-girt plain ;
Loud-swelling anthems sang the praise of God,
Our full-toned voices thundered out the words
That Moses heard on Sinai from the Lord ;
And oft at eve our grey-haired seers would tell
Of those two mightiest prophets, Israel's pride,
Chariots and horsemen, strong to save or slay,
The Tishbite, and the peasant, Shaphat's son,
From fair Meholah.   And the months passed on ;
We sowed and reaped, we planted and we built,
Working and praying, till the toil became
Itself a worship.   Words of mystic power
Came from my lips, when o'er me poured the flood
Of surging sound, the rushing, mighty wind
Sweeping the chords of life, and stirring thoughts
That must find utterance.   And I dreamt my
        dream
Of honoured age, the crown of honoured life ;
I saw myself, my white hairs flowing down,
The snowy mantle reaching to my feet,
And round me gathered all the prophet-band
That owned me as their master ; and I stood,

The head and leader of their glorious praise,
As Samuel stood of old.

              And now I sit,
All lonely, homeless, weary of my life,
Thick darkness round me, and the stars all dumb,
That chanted erst their wondrous tale of joy.
And thou hast done it all, O faithless one!
O Gomer! whom I loved as never wife
Was loved in Israel, all the wrong is thine!
Thy hand hath spoilèd all my tender vines,
Thy foot hath trampled all my pleasant fruits,
Thy sin hath laid my honour in the dust.
Men throw the blame on me, they mock my grief;
They wondered at my choice, and whispered
     words—
"The prophet woo the harlot!"—told their scorn.
They saw in me the poor, weak victim-fool
Of beauty's power to bow the strongest will,
To taint the purest, drive the wisest mad.
Yet call I God to witness, not from pulse
Of sensuous passion thrilling through the veins,
Or love of outward beauty, sought I thee,
And won thee as my bride.   Nor charge I thee
With feignèd semblance of a blameless life,
The eyes cast down, and veilèd cheeks that flush,
When looks admiring tell their power to charm.
Not blinded or deceived I made my choice;
I knew thy alien blood, thy wanton heart;

I saw the morning of thy youth defiled ;
I watched thee, when the summer sun went down,
And in the purple gleamed the silvery moon
Walking in brightness, join the priestess-throng
In mystic dance, thy timbrel in thy hand,
Thy bright eyes flashing fire, thy streaming hair
O'er neck and bosom falling, all thy soul
Bound by the wild enchantment ; and I knew
What followed on the revel, and for grief
And shame I wept.   " So fallen, yet so young !
So fair and bright ! so stained, polluted, vile ! "
And sorrow passed to pity, pity grew
To yearning love.   To seek and save the lost,
To call thee mine, and bring thee back to God,
Became the master-passion of my heart,
Forgetful of my calling and my fame :
And never in the hour when rushing streams
Of light from Heaven have flooded all my soul,
Or clear, low whispers from the Eternal Word
Have pointed out my path, have I believed
More firmly that my will was one with God's,
His oracle my one unerring guide,
Than in that hour when all my heart was thine.

And so I wooed thee, and thou didst not spurn
The prophet's offered love.¹   Awhile there woke
Within thy soul the thoughts of nobler life,
And so thou call'dst me husband.   O my God !

Look Thou with pity on me, as I track
That fearful past.   Renouncing all the joys,
The blessings of the bridegroom and the bride,
When each to other brings the virgin heart,
The Eden-bliss of lilies white and pure,
The stainless passion purifying sense,
I, knowing all, enfolded in mine arms
A lily torn and trampled in the mire,
A poor crushed dove, its snow-white beauty gone.
     And soon the canker spread.   The prophet's
          home,
The simple life of labour and of prayer,
The sabbath-gathering, and the new moon's feasts,
These grew distasteful.   All her wayward heart
Went back to those wild dances of the night,
The garland, and the music, and the song ;
And soon the wish impelled her to the act ;
She trod that path again.   She turned from me,
Her husband and her lord, and took her place
Once more among the slaves of Ashtaroth,
And did as others did.   Oh ! bitterest grief,
Oh ! darkest hour in all a father's life,
When, listening to the cry of new-born babes,
The warring currents ebb and flow within,
One impulse true and godlike, all the love
Of sire to son full streaming through his soul,
And one of doubt and fear.   I dared not call
Those babes mine own ; and dared I clasp the fruit

Of that abhorred transgression ?   So I turned
As, year by year, three births in order came,
Year after year, in sorrow and in wrath ;
And when the eighth day shone, with mystic names,
I told the secret sorrow of my soul ;
Jezreel, my first-born, witness of a guilt
As foul as was the blood on Jehu's hand,
Lo-Ammi, Lo-Ruhamah, "not mine own,"
" No yearning of my soul goes forth to thee."

   The children grew ; they smiled their infant
      smiles ;
They lisped with prattling whispers, and they called
Me "father ;" and my heart was bowed with woe.
At eve I sat, and watched them as they slept,
With gentler thoughts.   " Plead with your mother,
      plead,
O children ! whom I cherish as mine own ;
I change your names, and cancel all the curse
Which shut you out from love.   Oh, let your voice
Break through the spell that holds her in its chains;
Your baby-fingers touch her hardened heart,
Win back her wandering fancy, make her true,
And pure, and faithful.   So a happier glow
May yet surround the sunset of my life ;
And age may come to find me circled round
With loving wife, dear children, honouring friends.
Far better ending than my youth's vain dreams,

Far nobler blessing than the crown of praise
Which waits for him who leads the white-robed
    choir."

    It might not be.   To depths of lower shame
She sank all heedless.   In her frenzied guilt,
Leaving the one true guardian of her life,
She sought another's home.   With him she dwelt,
In guilty snatches of delirious joy,
Drowning in sin all memory of the past,
Bewitched by evil, till the flame burnt out,
As burn the thorns that sparkle on the hearth,
And left her cold and shivering in the gloom.
The adulterer's love, grown weary, turned to hate,
And bitter words made way for brutal deed ;
And dragging her, once fondled and caressed,
As men may drag a slave they take in war,
Before the men who gather in the gate,
He offered her for money, less for greed
Of gold or silver, than in scorn and hate,
To grieve her woman's soul with foulest shame,
The lowest price demanding that men ask
For boy half-grown, or woman past her prime,
Half money, half in kind ; and none would buy.
But I was there, and, weeping blinding tears,
I took her to myself, and paid the price
(Strange contrast to the dowry of her youth
When first I wooed her) ; and she came again

To dwell beneath my roof. Yet not for me
The tender hopes of those departed years
And not for her the freedom and the love
I then bestowed so freely. Sterner rule
Is needed now : in silence and alone,
In shame and sorrow, wailing, fast, and prayer,
She must blot out the stains that made her life
One long pollution. I, too, must abide
The issue of that penance, suffering long,
Her friend, yet not her husband, till the work
Be done, and all the wanton soul and sense
Be chastened into pureness. And as yet
The tears come not, but sullen, angry frown,
And fear that turns to hate, rejecting love,
And misery that crushes out the hope,
Each evil passion rushing through the soul,
And making life a hell. Ah me ! my God !
Why was I born to taste this depth of woe?
Why closed not darkness o'er my infant life
On that accursèd day when joyful lips,
Unknowing of the future, raised the cry,
" Rejoice, O mother ! Lo ! a child is born "?

And yet through all the mystery of my years
There runs a purpose which forbids that wail
Of passionate despair. I have not lived
At random, as a soul whom God forsakes ;
But evermore His Spirit led me on,

Prompted each purpose, taught my lips to speak,
Stirred up within me that deep love, and now
Reveals the inner secret. I have learnt,
Poor, weak, and frail, to love the fallen soul
Of one thus worthless. I have given my peace,
My honour, yea, my life for her who turns
Unthankful from me. Is there not a cause?
Hath not our God wooed Israel as His bride,
The stubborn, wayward Israel, in His love
And pity, pardoning all the sins of old?
And here, too, all is baseness. Crimes of sense,
And crimes of spirit, tainting heart and life,
The altars, and the incense, and the songs
With which she bowed to Baalim; the lust,
The rapine, and the hate that rose to heaven:
These, these have lit the fire of righteous wrath;
And He, the jealous God, will visit sins
Of fathers upon children. I have learnt,
In this sharp teaching of an inward woe,
The meaning of that jealousy. I know
The pity, and the sorrow, and the pain,
The love which waters cannot quench, the zeal
Which does not shrink from chastening. So it is,
And equal stripes must fall on equal sin.
She sits alone, that poor self-widowed one,
Bowed down to earth. No golden circlet now
Crowns her dark locks. No Tyrian purple pours
Its rich, soft folds around the marble limbs;

No pearls or rubies glow on either arm ;
The topaz and the sapphire cease to blend
Their radiance on the anklet's dainty band,
The coronet of feet that scorned for pride
The earth they trod on. Reft of pomp and state,
Her brow deep-furrowed with a wrath suppressed,
And lips that tell of sullen, inward storm,
She bides her time ; and I must leave her there
Till those dark clouds have melted into tears,
And heart of stone gives way to heart of flesh.
The time is long and weary, and I sigh
For very grief as mournful days pass on ;
And yet no sorrow, no repentant prayer,
No craving for forgiveness speaks of change.
And thou, O Israel, thou must bear thy doom,
Grow old and fail, in homes that are not thine,
Where mighty rivers water lands unknown,
And Asshur's palaces, in pride of strength,
Rise high upon the banks of Hiddekel.
No glory of the past shall wait thee there,
No pomp of kings, no priests in gorgeous robes,
No victims bleeding on the altar-fires ;
Nor shall the ephod set with sparkling gems,
Nor pillar speaking of the gate of heaven,
Nor Teraphim with strange mysterious gleams,
Give then their signs oracular. Long years
Thy sons shall hang their harps on Babel's trees,
And wander homeless over all the lands,

A by-word to the nations, till at last
The door of hope is opened, and the light
Breaks in on that thick darkness.   But the end
Is certain.   They will turn and seek their God,
Seek David's son, the heir of David's throne,
No longer hardened in their scorn of scorn,
But mourning, weeping, seeking peace from God,
Renewing once again the primal love,
The day of those espousals when the King
Chose his young bride from out the desert world,
And claimed her as His own.   Oh, boundless joy !
Oh, day long looked for ! worth the price we pay,
The penalty of exile, hunger, shame,
If only it may come in all its peace,
In brightness as the morning.

                    So I sit,
Feeding on thoughts that circle round from grief,
To highest gladness : so I judge their faults,
Mark out their sentence, that adulterous wife,
That more adulterous people.   Yet there comes,
To bring me low, the question, " What am I,
That I should sit in judgment ?   This my woe,
That rends the air with passionate complaint,
Bears that no witness of a guilt like theirs,
A penalty as needful ?"   Through my soul
There thrills the trembling shame that whelms the
       heart
Of woman faithless.   Thou, my soul, wast loved,

As bride by bridegroom, by the Eternal Lord ;
And thou, too, hast been false. Thy will has turned
To dreams of self. Thy work beguiled thy soul
With wanton longings for the prophet's fame,
The power to move the terror or the love
Of listening thousands. Not the word of peace,
The free glad tidings from the Lord of Life
To thousand way-worn wanderers in their grief,
But battle, strife, contention, with the kings,
The priests, the prophets, who opposed thy will,—
This led thee on. The heart of all thy love
To that poor sinner was thy pride of strength,
Secret of all thy failure. Thou hast said,
" I in my might will be as God, and bring
Good out of evil, sway the tides of life,
Avenge the wrong, chastise each secret sin ;"
And so thou could'st not win thy heart's desire,
Wast powerless through thy dream of fancied
      strength,
Wast baffled by an evil like thine own :
Thou too must sit in ashes ; on thy lips
Must be the seal of silence. Thou must learn
Thy guilt in its full measure ; thou must own
Thy need of cleansing. Only when thine arm
In sense of weakness reaches forth to God,
Wilt thou be strong to suffer and to do ;
Only when thou shalt yield thy will to His,
Renouncing self's vain dreams, and take thy place

Among the lowest, shall thy power return
To speak His word, to bow men's hearts to Him.
Till then sit thou without the prophet's garb,
And utter thou no oracle of God ;
Low on the earth, in dust and ashes bowed,
Learn from the outcast, count thyself as vile,
Taste in thine heart the bitterness of death,
Plunge thy whole life within the dark abyss,
And then thou too shalt, after many days,
Turn in thine anguish to the Eternal Lord,
And, wearied out with evil, seeking peace,
Dwell in His Goodness everlastingly.

June, 1864.

THE HOUSE OF THE RECHABITES.

I.

JEHONADAB.

" And when Jehu was departed thence, he lighted on Jehonadab the son of
Rechab coming to meet him : and he saluted him, and said to him, Is thine
heart right, as my heart is with thy heart ? "—2 KINGS x. 15.

THE shadows fall : before mine eyes there
    floats
The thick, black darkness. Ere my voice is hushed,
I fain would see you gather round my tent,
And speak my parting counsels. Ye, my sons,
The glory of the spring-tide of my years,
Warriors of God, whom I have watched in youth
Outrun the wild goat to the topmost crag,
Plunge into Jordan when the harvest flood
O'erflows its banks, and, battling with the stream,
Rise up victorious on the further shore,
Whose faces, scarred and seamed in many a fight,
Showed noblest hearts, all ignorant of fear ;
And ye, who not by bonds of natural birth,
But sworn obedience, one in life and heart,

H

Have chosen me your father, whom I own
As sons of Rechab ; come ye, one and all,
Men, women, children, hear the words of one
Who speaks as God has taught him.   Through the
    years
Those words shall dwell with you for weal or woe,
Blessing or cursing.   On your heads the vow
Shall rest for ever.   Not for you the life
Of sloth and ease within the city's gates,
Where idol-feasts are held, and incense smokes
To Baalim and Ashtaroth ; where man
Loses his manhood, and the scoffers sit
Perverting judgment, selfish, soft, impure :
Not yours the task of those that sow and reap,
Or plant the olive and the vine.   Ye dwell,
Free as, of old, your fathers roamed the lands,
When Joshua led their hosts, and, Canaan won,
Gave them their lot in Israel.   Still ye wend
From hill to hill, with camels and with sheep,
Asses and oxen, and your tents are seen
Outspread upon the pleasant Gilead land,
Blackened, yet comely.   And the Nazarite's oath
Is still upon you.   Not for you the cup
That sparkles with the crimson blood of grapes :
The wine that glads the heart of man and God
Ye may not taste.   The wild, entrancing thrill
That stirs the veins with pulse of warm desire,
And swells the voice of song, and bids the feet

Move to blithe music in exulting dance,—
Leave this to lower natures.   Ye have seen
The poison at its work, have watched the soul
Lose calmness, strength, and wisdom, rising high
To sink down low, all brutish, in the abyss
Where man forgets his God.   But ye, the true,
The faithful, bound, as servants of the Lord,
With heart and strength to serve Him, stand ye
          fast,
Nor cloud your spirits with the fleshly taint,
Nor join in revel at the idol-feasts,
Nor turn your backs in craven fear of death.

    Dark were the days when first within my soul
The stirrings of a message from the Lord
Woke, half-unfelt.   The house of Omri trod
Its evil path, and Ahab's alien queen,
Priestess of Baal, swore to crush our faith.
The prophets of Jehovah died their death,
Or stoned, or sawn asunder, or in caves
By tens and fifties hid themselves for fear ;
And Baal's altars smoked on every height,
And Baal's black-robed priests in every town
Took tithes and offerings ; and by moonlight pale,
In shadowy groves, to Ashtaroth their queen,
Fair maidens danced adoring.   Then the drought
Fell on us, and the famine ; and the sky
Glared on us like a molten heaven of brass ;

And the earth gaped for weariness and thirst;
And parchèd lips cursed God for pain of heart.
  And then the Tishbite came. His long, black
    hair
Flowed round him like a mantle, and he stood
On Carmel's height, and all day long the priests
Called on their god, and cut themselves with knives,
And poured their blood, and raised their cries in
    vain.
But when he prayed, as sank the westering sun,
The fire descended, and the wondering crowd
No longer halted, wavering between two,
Baal or Jehovah.   Quivering, pale, dismayed,
Faint with the sickness of a hope deferred,
The priests and prophets of the stranger god
Were seized and slaughtered; and the torrent's bed,
Where water long had failed, now filled with blood,
Ran crimson to the sea.   And then the cloud
Rose in the west, a speck of blackness, small
As is this hand, yet spreading fast and far,
With sound of many waters, and the rush
Of darkening tempest; and the glad showers fell,
And earth revived, and all the streamlets sang,
With joyful voices, and the mightier floods
Swept on and on exulting.
                    Yet awhile
Deliverance came not.   Still the foul disease
Remained, unhealed; and Ahab's evil ways

Cried to the Heavens for vengeance.   Faint and
        sad,
Weary of life, as one who stands alone,
The last survivor of a fallen faith,
Elijah fled to Horeb.   None may know
The mystery of that vision on the mount,
The fire, the earthquake, and the whirlwind; last,
The still small voice.   And soon the vengeance fell
On Ahab and his house.   We heard afar
The deed of wrong, the tyrant's fond desire,
The vineyard seized, and Naboth foully slain,
The last, great guilt that filled the o'erflowing cup ;
And then it came.   The chance-drawn bow smote
        down
The coward king who sought to 'scape disguised,
And dogs licked up his blood in Jezreel.
Of all the prophet's words none fell to earth
Fruitless and vain, and though his course was run,
And soon he left us, in the fiery car
Mounting to brighter skies of Paradise,
Himself an army, stay of all our hopes,
The chariot and the horseman of our strength,
Our father and our guide, the years fulfilled
Each slighted warning.   Shame, disgrace, and death
Poured down in quick succession, and our hearts
Rejoiced to think deliverance near at hand.
But most I joy to live those hours again,
When Nimshi's son had wrought his deed of doom,

And Ahab's sons, and queenly Jezebel,
Lay low in dust.   All flushed with pride and zeal,
He met us in his chariot.   I was there
With you, my sons, and over all the hills
Our tents were scattered, and our myriad sheep
Came to their shearing, and our warriors tried
Made up an army.   And the new-made king
Knew how to use us.   Israel's king, I say,
In all the pride of conquest, sought to clasp
My hand in friendship, though of alien blood,
And half of alien creed (for Jehu still
Bowed down before the golden calves that stood
In Bethel and in Dan); and now, behold,
We rode together, I, the Kenite chief,[1]
And he, the king.   And over all the land
Went forth the summons, " Come, ye priests, that serve
    serve
At Baal's altars.   Come ye, all who bow
At Baal's shrine.   The king will hold a feast,
And offer up a mightier sacrifice
Than Ahab ever dreamt of."   So they came,
From East and West, the false apostate crew,
From North and South, all striving, eager, hot,
To be among the foremost.   In they streamed,
In garments dyed with purple, such as come
From Tyrian looms; and soon the Temple-gates
Closed in upon the thronging, weltering crowd;
And then our moment came.   I gave the sign,

And ye, your bright swords flashing in the air,
Went in to do your work.   Not hand to hand,
In equal fight, not struggling hard for life,
But helpless, powerless, taken in the snare,
Ye found your victims, and with firm, fixed eye,
And hands unflinching till the wearied arm
Refused its office, slew, and slew, and slew
Your startled, trembling foes.   The red sun fell
On that red stream that gurgled past the walls,
And over pallid faces threw its gleam
Of ghastly brightness.   Ah, my soul leaps up
At that remembrance.   Not a whit behind
That sacrifice on Carmel, which I saw,
Was this my hands had wrought.   We crushed the snake
    snake
Our master bruised.   Remember, O my God,
That slaughter of Thy foes.   A whisper runs
(I know it) that some dreamer in his cell,
Who counts himself a prophet, has condemned
That deed of vengeance.[2]   Let him dream his dreams
    dreams
Of pitying love, and talk of curses dark
That rest upon that day of Jezreel,
And claim fulfilment.   New and strange to me
Such thoughts as these.   My soul was early trained
To smite and slay the haters of my God,
To use or tongue, or hand, or sword, or stone,
As each was fittest.   Who will blame my deed,

And spare Elijah's?   And if aught of wrong
Have mixed itself with either, Thou, O God,
Wilt pardon it as over-eager zeal.
The willing slave who does his lord's behest,
O'erstepping, here or there, the bounds of right,
In very strength of love which hates the foes
His Lord condemns, may claim the guerdon high
Of faithful service.   Thou, my King, my God,
Wilt own Thy servant, and my name shall live
As lives the name of Jehu, through the years,
Linked with that day of Jezreel.   Ye, my sons,
Shall make that name immortal.   Still your flocks
Shall feed on Gilead's hills, and in your tents
Ye and your sons shall dwell, and shall not taste
The purpling draught that maddens all the sense,
And numbs the soul; but still your food shall be
The curdled goat's milk, and the golden store
That drops, all fragrant, from the flinty rock,
And water clear and cool shall quench your thirst;
And so your days shall lengthen in the land,
As mine have lengthened.   Now I go my way
I know not whither, but my sleep is sweet,
Sweet as the night to him who all day long
Has chased the hart upon the mountain height;
And I pass on to where my fathers dwell,
Each in his rock-hewn couch; and I shall see
The prophets I have known, and they, I think,
Will give me welcome, and a change will come

O'er sense and spirit making all things clear :
And there, it may be, I shall see once more
The great Elijah, whom the fiery car
Bore from us, and shall greet him, as of old,
" My father, O my father, we thy sons,
Sons of the chariot of our Israel's strength.[3]
Still hold thy name in honour, do thy deeds,
And live thy life."   And then from out the clouds
His voice may answer, even as Jehu's did,
" Give me thine hand."   And I, who rode of yore
In Jehu's chariot, mounting higher yet
To greater glory, side by side may stand
(The angels round me, and the steeds of fire
Through golden clouds advancing to the Throne)
With him, the mightiest seer, till I, too, see
The King in all His beauty, and my voice
Joins in the shout of all the sons of God.

September, 1864.

II.

JAAZANIAH.

"Then I took Jaazaniah the son of Jeremiah, the son of Habaziniah, and his brethren, and all his sons, and the whole house of the Rechabites, and I brought them into the house of the Lord."—JEREM. xxxv. 3.

IT is not that our hearts have waxen faint,
   Or wills grown false. We blush not to confess
Our father's name, and still the vows we keep
By which he bound us.   But the times were hard ;
The great King's armies ravaged all the land,
Bitter and hasty, mad with lust and rage,
And all our flocks and herds they tore away,
Nor spared or infant smiling at the breast,
Or hoary-headed age.   And so we dwell
Within the city's walls, who, long years past,
Ne'er slept beneath a roof, but still in tents
Lived as our fathers lived.   We loathe the change :
The bright, keen air that swept the uplands wild,
Sweet with the fragrance of the fields of God,
We breathe no more ; but, stifling, dense, and
      thick,
Charged with the taint of pestilence and death,

Foul as the draught-house which, of olden time,
Reared its proud height exulting, as a shrine
Where Baal sat enthroned, which he, our sire,
The son of Rechab, stript of all its pride,
The city's vapours choke us. And our garb,
Our speech, our customs, all are put to shame ;
The revellers and the drunkards make their songs
Because we feast not with them, and they tempt
Our purer youth to stain their souls with sin ;
And, in the twilight, where the cross-ways meet,
The harlot-stranger greets them with her wiles,
And lures them to the chambers of the dead ;
And so the cry goes up, as once it went
From Admah and Zeboim, and the cup
Fills evermore, till soon the wrath of God
Shall overflow in fury. Base and foul
This life of cities : now we see and know
The wisdom of the oath that bade us shun
And hate it evermore.
     And yet we found
E'en there a remnant, faithful friends and true,
Servants of God, and all our hearts leapt up,
When through the Temple's gates, and stately courts,
We passed adoring. Not till then our eyes
Had looked on that full splendour, nor our ears
Heard the clear trumpets which the priests of God
Blow loud and long, or that great shout of praise,
When Hallelujah from the white-robed choir

Rises on high, and thousand voices chant,
Re-echoing Hallelujah, wave on wave,
The sound of many waters.   All our days
Till now, when Sabbaths bade us rest from toil,
Or new-moon feast filled every soul with joy,
We gathered here or there, in tent or grove,
Where'er a prophet met us ; and we prayed,
And he declared his message, and we heard,
And so we went our way.   But now we tread
The courts of God, which He of old chose out
To set His Name there ; and the cedarn roof,
Fretted and bossed with gold of Ophir, carved
With all the workman's cunning, wins our gaze.
Here, where great David's greater son stood up,
And prayed his prayer ; where, bright and lustrous,
        shone
The glory of the Presence, sapphire gleams
And amber brightness, blent with orient rays
Of amethyst and emerald ; here to kneel,
And watch the thousand pilgrims as they pass,
And see the sheep and oxen, flocks and herds,
Driven to the altars,—this is joy, indeed ;
And fain our steps would tread the hallowed way,
And fain our voice would swell the surging praise,
And rather would we stay to keep the doors,
And sweep the pavement of the House of God,
Than dwell where all the proud ones in their tents
Exult in conquest.

Not in vain that wish :
They welcomed us, the prophets and the priests,
As friends and brothers, and with open hearts
Gave all we needed.   Chief among them all,
Stood forth the pale, sad seer of Anathoth,
The man of many woes, whose gleaming eyes
Told of a fire still burning, and whose lips
Now slow and feeble, now of mightiest speech,
Made known the thoughts of God.   He owned
          in us
A kindred life, for he, too, dwelt apart,
An exile from his own, and would not tread
The house of feasting ; and at him they scoffed
Who scoffed at us, and evermore they cried,
" Lo ! the mad prophet : hear him rave again."

One morn he came to us.   The prophet's hour
Was on him ; not with common speech, or mien
Of wonted calmness, but in heat of soul,
With clear, fixed eye, and voice that whispered low,
As one on whom the hand of God weighs hard,
He spake his will, and bade me follow him
With all my father's house.   Through gate and
          court
He led the way to where the eastern tower
Looks down on Kidron.   There the chamber stands
Where Hanan's followers gather up the words
Their Master speaks, and there he bade us stay ;

And then from out the treasure of the House
He brought the golden goblets chased of old
By Hiram's workmen (such as 'scaped the spoil
When Shishak plundered), crusted thick with gems,
Embossed and graven.   Wine he brought, the best
That Eshcol's vineyards boast of, sweet and bright,
And, pouring, bade us drink.   Yes, he, the seer,
The prophet of the Lord, stood forth to tempt,
As Satan tempts.   To break the vows of God,
To do dishonour to our father's name,
To taste the cup those dying lips had cursed ;—
To this he called us.   Wondering eyes we turned,
All startled at the suddenness of change,
But yield we might not.   No, nor prophet's voice,
Nor angel's message floating through the air,
Nor lengthened skill and subtlety of speech
Might bend us from our purpose.   So we told
Our simple tale.   " The oath of God was strong,
Stronger than all things else.   Our souls were
        bound
To keep our father's hest.   Stern need alone
Had driven us from our tents, but all the rest
We still obeyed."   " Oh, ask us not to taste,
Thou prophet of the Lord, lest we too fall
Beneath the curse."
                    And then the mystery cleared ;
Not luring us to sin, but trusting well
Our strong obedience, he would find in us

A pattern unto Israel.   We had kept
Our father's word, but Judah had been false,
And Israel frail.   In vain the Lord had sent
His prophets, rising early ; and in vain
Had pleaded with His children.   Therefore came
On us the blessing, and on them the doom :
For them a city captured, homes destroyed,
A life of exile ; and for-us the praise
Which God, not man, awards to faithful souls,
A name to live through all the age to come ;
Yea, more than all, beyond our hope or dream,
The words went forth that met our heart's desire ;—
" The son of Rechab shall not want a man
To stand before my face for evermore." [4]
As stand the sons of Aaron when, in robes
Of linen white and clean, they tread the courts,
Or wave the incense,—as the Levites stand,
Choir facing choir, and chant their hymns at night,
Through the still darkness breathing praise to God,
To cheer the watchman on his lonely round,
The soldier on his turret ; so shall we
Dwell, night and day, within the holy house
Which God has called his own : our lips shall bring
        bring
Their daily offering, and our hands shall sweep
The strings of harp or psaltery.   Pure and cleansed,
The chosen band of Nazarites shall own
Our tried endurance.   In the months to come,

Or few, or many, we shall find our home,
As finds the swallow, in the courts of God.

And if the days are dark, and doom of woe
Hangs o'er us; if the dread Chaldæan scourge
Shall sweep the land and leave it desolate;
If cedar beams and carvèd roof shall burn,
And columns lie, all shattered, in the dust;
And golden vessels serve for idol-feasts,
And all the music of the choirs be hushed,
And groans and curses rend the startled air;—
If, exiles wandering on Euphrates' banks,
We hang our harps upon the pale, grey trees,
Whose weeping branches plash the wide, waste
    flood,
And, when they bid us, in their mirth and pride,
Sing at their feasts the chief of Zion's songs,[5]
Make answer, " How in this strange land and drear
Can hallowed songs, the hymns of God, be ours?"
And then in speech they know not, breathe our
    soul,
Cursing, not blessing:—if all this shall come
On us and on our children, still our hearts
Shall live in hope. The word is sure and fixed
As are the everlasting hills of God,
And still the sons of Rechab shall not fail
To stand before the Lord; and still their feet
Shall tread His courts, their voices speak His praise.

And thou, O Prophet, Seer of Anathoth,
Shalt see, in vision, all thy word fulfilled ;
And the old order, waxing dim, shall pass
Away before the new, and words of God
Written on fleshly tablets of the heart,
Shall win from all obedience, trust, and love.
So all thy woes shall end, thy restless grief
ᴊhall rest at last, and near the throne of God
Thou still shalt stand, and for thy people pray,
Thy grey hairs crowned with glory;⁶ while, on
        earth,
The sons of Rechab treasure up thy words,
And live, expectant of the mightier time,
When He, the Lord our Righteousness, shall come,
And call His people from the East and West
To dwell for ever in the Eternal Light,
At rest within the Paradise of God.

September, 1864.

III.

JAMES THE JUST.

" But whilst they were thus stoning him, one of the priests of the sons of
Rechab the sons of Rechabim, who are mentioned by the prophet Jeremiah,
cried, ' Stop, what do ye, the Just One prays for you.' "—HEGESIPPUS, in *Euseb.*
Hist. Ecc. ii. 23.

YOU ask me, friend, the story of my life,
    How came it that for years I held my peace,
Half-doubting, half-believing, went my way,
And did my work, as if the Nazarene
Had never taught, or died, or risen again ;
Whilst thou, e'er yet the stir and rush were o'er
Of that great Pentecost, as fully His,
Did'st join the Galileans. So thy path
Was taken, and it parted us. For thee,
No longer, service in the Temple's courts,
Slaying oxen, burning incense, but the work
To spread thy Lord's good tidings o'er the world
To Jew or Gentile, visiting the sick,
Clothing the naked, gauging earth's abyss
Of hopeless sorrow, where in dungeons foul
Men curse their God, or fret their loathsome lives
In galleys or in mines, and still in each

Uplifting high the Cross on which thy self
Was crucified with Christ. And now we meet,
The long years ended like a tale that's told,
And never more shall clouds of incense float
To gilded rafters, never more shall eye
Of wondering traveller glance from height to height,
And count those towers of Zion. Low in dust
They lie, those goodly columns, and the fire
Has charred the sculptured cedar, and the song
Is turned to wailing. Yes, we meet again ;
And I, the doubter, faltering, half-convinced,
Am one with thee in heart, and faith, and life,
Call Christ my Lord, and seek to make Him mine.
" How was it ? " I will tell thee. Long ago
(Thou mind'st the time), when yet the gathering down
Grew on my youthful cheek, and first I took
My place among the Levites in their choir,
There came a rumour that the hour had come,
Long hoped-for, long deferred, when God should
    raise
A prophet unto Israel. Stiff and cold,
And poor and dead the teaching of our scribes,
Hillel and Shammai, vexing all our souls
With grievous burdens, telling o'er again
Their thrice-told tales. And all our hearts leapt up
At this good news. The Spirit had not failed,
The Lord's arm was not shortened. Once again
The Word had come, and he, the Baptist, stood

As stood of old, Elijah.   We were sent,
Levites and priests, to test the preacher's claim,
And search his teaching.   Others came away,
Hating or scorning, " He is mad," they said,
" A demon holds him.   Here is one of us,
A priest as we are, and he lives a life
That shames us, turns away from all his friends,
From feasts, and song, and garments soft and rich,
The honours of the priesthood and the scribes,
And makes his dwelling in the wilderness,
And lives on locusts like the wandering sons
Of Ishmael, and will rob the wild bee's store,
And drink the stream that gushes from the rock."
   So they in scorn and wonder, but my soul
Went forth to him, admiring.   Here I found
A life which bore on every lineament
The stamp of that old greatness which our sire,
The son of Rechab, bade us strive to keep,
Age after age.   Elijah walked again
This earth of ours : and half I could have deemed
The Christ had come in him, but prophets old
Forbade the thought, and told of David's seed
And David's city, and himself confessed,
" I am not he, the Anointed, whom ye seek,"
And told us of another yet to come
Whom then we knew not.

                    Soon we knew too well :
The people's rumours took another turn,

Another prophet rose, and mighty deeds,
Wrought by His hands, proclaimed Him more than
      John ;
And mighty words were spoken, and there ran,
From peasants by the fair Tiberias' lake,
Yea, among priests and scribes who feared to speak,
The whisper, " This is Christ." My soul was stirred
To question further : and I saw the man,
Found much to love, admire, do homage to,
And but for one thing perfect. But the flaw
Seemed fatal. He, the Galilean prophet, came
Eating and drinking, as the sons of men
Eat flesh, drink wine. He mingled with the feasts,
Where men make merry : yea, He gave the wine,
Put forth His power to give it, copious store
To last a twelvemonth. Could I trust in one
Who stooped to this ? Or could I faithless prove
To all my fathers, cast aside their life
As vain self-torture, profitless, and poor,
The bondage of a time of ignorance,
Now gone for ever ? So I held my peace,
Half-pitying, half-admiring, waiting on
To see the issue. Then they worked their will,
Annas and Caiaphas, and the slave-like crew
That look to Cæsar ; and the prophet hung,
All stript and bleeding, on the accursèd cross
And then, we heard, He rose. The rumour ran
Through Tyropœon up the Temple steps,

Passed on from priest to priest, " The man ye slew
Is risen from the dead." It might be so ;
They spoke it bravely, those, the faltering friends
Who once forsook Him. Now they did not doub*
Were not faint-hearted, stood before the Scribes,
The Priests, the Elders, constant in their tale ;
And thou, friend, did'st believe them ; but for me
The old doubt was not cleared. They also drank
The wine we may not taste. From hand to hand
They passed the cup, memorial of their Lord,
Bond of their union. None might join their sect
Except he drank it. But I might not drink,
And therefore could not join : and still I said,
As once Gamaliel spoke in full debate,
" God will make clear His purpose ; I, at least,
Can wait in silence."

                        So the years passed on :
Ere long I marked each day within our courts,
A Nazarite form, in linen pure and white,
As each set service summoned men to prayer,
Still at the third hour, and the sixth, and ninth,
As one to whom the Temple was a home ;
Pale, calm, and worn with fasting, there he stood,
And never costly oil bedewed his brow,
And never wine-cup touched the saintly lips,
Save, it might be, one drop, the merest sign
The token of his brotherhood in Christ.
Silent he was, and gentle, never word

Of anger 'scaped him.   Here was one, indeed,
Our father Jonadab would own as his,
One whom I might admire, and seek to make
His heart as my heart.   And this man, they said,
Was Jacôb, brother of the Crucified,
Once doubting as we doubted, now convinced
By what he saw, and owning now no more
The fleshly kindred, seeing on the Throne
His brother, all men's brother.   And the priests
Gave him free entry, would not turn him back,
Threw open all the gates.   They knew the man
And bowed before his spotlessness of life,
And thought the risk less great to let him pass,
Seeing how gentle, worn, subdued he stood,
Than cause an uproar.   But at last their wrath
Was kindled : blinded in their rage, they seized
Their victim, and, mistaking all his life,
Unknowing all the steadfastness of soul
That slumbered, waiting for its hour to come,
They urged confession.   "Speak, thou Just One,
          speak ;
Thou knew'st the Nazarene, whose followers speak
Blaspheming words against our Holy Place,
As against Moses.   Thou hast never joined
In aught our law forbids.   Thy lips are free
From all pollution.   Zealous for the law,
We honour thee as one more zealous still,
True to the death.   Well then, be bold at last,

To disavow the leader, as in act
Thou joinest not the followers. Speak one word,
The word which parts thee from the Name we hate,
And then thou shalt be ours for evermore ;
And much we will concede thee, highest place,
And priestly honours, yea, and priestly robes."
    And so they led him where the Temple's tower
Looks down o'er Kidron, and from either court
They gazed, expectant : and, at last, he spake :
" Ye slayers of the Just One, I have prayed,
As prayed my Master, that this hour might pass,
And leave you guiltless, prayed that ye might turn,
Believe, and live ; but, lo ! ye will not hear.
Your blood be on your head ; my soul is free :
I bear my witness.   Know ye, all who hear,
How from my heart I worship Him ye slew,
No longer as my brother, but my Lord,
Yea, as my King, my God.   The stainless life
I knew long since, the mighty deeds of love ;
Yet still I wavered.   But, at last, there came
The victory over doubt.   These eyes have seen
Risen from the dead the brother whom I knew ;
And now I know Him, mighty to redeem,
As wise to teach.   I hear His footstep's fall
Through all the world's wild clamour.   At the door
He stands and knocks, and pleads, and calls in vain,
And soon will come as Judge.   The cry goes up
To Heaven, and all the martyr-souls, that wait

Beneath the altar, shout, nor shout in vain,
'How long, O Lord, how long!' And then the
    End :
This Temple where I worship day and night,
Shall stream with blood of men, and desolate
With that abomination dark and dread,
Accursed of God, and trampled on by men,
Shall sink in flames. And then the hour shall come,
When shadows, types, and symbols falling off,
That sheathed the truth and hid it, all shall know
The mystery of the Kingdom.   Greek and Jew,
The seed of Japhet, and the sons of Shem,
And Ham's swarth brood shall offer up their prayer,
And all alike be heard.   The middle wall
Is broken down, and God's great love expands
Beyond the utmost sea."
                    Thus far he spake ;
The rest wild yells cut off. They gnashed their
    teeth,
They tore their garments, cursed, and spat on him ;
And then a moment's pause, and then a rush,
And we who stood below beheld his form
Fall headlong.   On the Temple stones he lay,
All bruised and bleeding ; but life still was there,
And slow, faint words came forth from quivering lips,
" Father, forgive them."   Then a giant form
Strode through the crowd, and with a fuller's club
(The man was one of those who do their work

Down by En-rogel) gave the final stroke,
And all was over.   Then my soul was moved;
The fire was kindled.   I had waited long
For truth to silence doubt, and now it came,
The token that I craved for.   This man's life
Was one long worship.   He who died this death,
Bearing this witness, had not lived a lie;
The hope that gave him strength, the love that
        taught
With good to conquer evil, were no dreams,
No vision of the night, no idle tale;
And therefore I believed: And so I spake,
"O fools, and blind.   The blood ye shed will cry
From out the earth for vengeance.   Once again
Ye slay the Just One.   Lo, the cup is full,
The wine is mixed, the wine of God's great wrath,
And ye shall drink it even to the dregs:
I flee for refuge from that wrath to come
To Him, the One deliverer.   All the past
I count but loss, if I may gain but that:
The place of honour in the Levites' chair,
The blessing that the sons of Rechab boast,
The long descent through lineage undefiled,
The vow that binds us to our father's name,
All these I cast aside to win but Thee,
Thou Christ of God."
                            They heard; the cries,
Redoubled, rose.   They led me to the gates;

They laid upon my head the dark, dire curse,
And sent me forth Anathema.   Alone,
Homeless, dishonoured, reft of name and fame,
I hid myself by day, and wandered forth
When evening fell, not knowing where I went ;
But through the shadow and the darkness shone
The presence of the Christ ; and all night long
The heavens were opened.   And the angels came,
Descending, rising, passing to and fro ;
The lonely slope of Olivet became
A house of God, the very gate of Heaven ;
And in the morn they welcomed me, the friends
Whom now I saw as angels, one in heart
And soul, and, all regardless of the curse
The priests had spoken, gave me rest and food.
They washed me in the stream that cleanses sin,
They broke the bread, and poured the wine or
   Christ ;
And so I call thee brother ; so old ties
Are knit again more closely, and our lives,
Long time divided, meet for evermore,
And we are priests within the Eternal Home,
The Temple of the City of our God.

September, 1864.

THREE CUPS OF COLD WATER.

I.

THE princely David, with his outlaw-band,
    Lodged in the cave Adullam. Wild and fierce,
With lion-like faces, and with eagle eyes,
They followed where he led. The danger pressed,
For over all the land the Philistines
Had spread their armies. Through Rephaim's vale
Their dark tents mustered thick, and David's home,
His father's city, Bethlehem, owned them lords.
'Twas harvest, and the crops of ripening corn
They ravaged, and with rude feet trampled down
The tender vines. Men hid themselves for fear
In woods or caves. The brave undaunted few,
Gathering round David, sought the mountain hold.
The sun was hot, and all day long they watched
With spear in hand and never-resting eye,
As those who wait for battle; but at eve
The eye grew dim, the lips were parched with
      thirst,
And from that arid rock no trickling stream

Of living water gushed.   From time-worn skins
The tainted drops were poured, and fevered lips
Half-loathing drank them up.   And David's soul
Was weary; the hot simoom scorched his veins;
The strong sun smote on him, and, faint and sick,
He sat beneath the shadow of the rock:
And then before his eyes a vision came,
Cool evening, meadows green, and pleasant sounds
Of murmuring fountains.   Oft in days of youth,
When leading home his flocks as sunset fell,
That fount had quenched his thirst, and dark-eyed
        girls,
The pride and joy of Bethlehem, meeting there,
Greeted the shepherd boy, their chieftain's son,
(As, bright and fair with waving locks of gold,
Exulting in the flush of youth's full glow,
He mingled with their throng), and gazing, rapt
With wonder at his beauty, gave him drink.
And now the words came feebly from his lips,
A murmur half in silence, which the ear
Of faithful followers caught: "Ah! who will bring
From that fair stream, which flowing by the gate
Of Bethlehem's wall makes music in the ear,
One drop to cool this tongue?"   They heard, the
        three,
The mightiest of the thirty, swift of foot
As are the harts upon the mountains, strong
As are the lions down by Jordan's banks;

They heard and darted forth ; down rock and crag
They leapt, as leaps the torrent on its course ;
Through plain and vale they sped, and never stayed,
Until the wide encampment of the foe
Warned them of danger nigh.   But not for fear
Abandoned they their task.   When evening fell,
And all the Philistines were hushed in sleep,
And over all the plain the full, bright moon
Poured its rich lustre, onward still they stole,
By tent fires creeping with hushed breath, and feet
That feared to wake the echoes, till at last
They heard the babbling music, and the gleam
Of rippling moonlight caught their eager eye,
And o'er them fell the shade of Bethlehem's gate.
They tarried not.   One full delicious draught
Slaked their fierce thirst, and then with anxious
        haste
They filled their water-urn, and full of joy,
They bore it back in triumph to their lord.
With quickened steps they tracked their path again
O'er plain and valley, up o'er rock and crag,
And as the early sunlight kissed the hills
They stood before him.   He had won their hearts
By brave deeds, gentle words, and stainless life ;
And now they came to give him proof of love,
And pouring out the water bade him drink.
But lo ! he would not taste.   He heard their tale
(In few words told, as brave men tell their deeds),

And lifting up his hands with solemn prayer,
As though he stood, a priest, before the shrine,
He poured it on the earth before the Lord.
" Far be it from me, God, that I should drink,
The slave of selfish lust, forgetting Thee,
Forgetting these my brothers.   In Thine eyes
This water fresh and cool is as the blood
Of hero-souls who jeopardied their lives :
That blood I may not taste.   As shrink the lips
From the hot life-stream of the Paschal Lamb,
So shrinks my soul from this.   To Thee, O Lord,
To Thee I pour it.   Thou wilt pardon me
For mine unkingly weakness, pardon them
For all rough deeds of war.   Their noble love
Shall cover all their sins ; for Thou hast claimed,
More than all blood of bulls and goats, the will
That, self-forgetting, lives in deeds like this."
    So spake the hero-king, and all the host
Looked on and wondered ; and those noble three,
The mightiest of the thirty, felt their souls
Knit closer to King David and to God.

II.

THROUGH wastes of sand the train of camels wound
Their lingering way.   The pilgrims, hasting on
To Mecca's shrine, were grieved and vexed at heart,

Impatient of delay.   The scorching sand
Lay hot and blinding round them, and the blast
Of sultry winds, as from a furnace mouth,
Brought blackness to all faces.   Whirling clouds
Of white dust filled their eyes, and, falling flat,
Crouching in fear, they waited till it passed.
Then, lifting up their eyes, there met their gaze
One fierce, hot glare, a waveless sea of sand.
No track of pilgrims' feet, nor whitening bones
Of camels or of asses, marked their way.
They wandered on, by sun and moon and stars
Guessing their path, not knowing where they went,
But Mecca's shrine they saw not.   Day by day,
Their scant stores scantier grew.   Their camels
          died;
No green oasis met their yearning eyes;
No rippling stream brought gladness to their hearts;
But glittering lakes that sparkled in the light,
Girt with the soft, green tufts of feathery palm,
Enticed them, hour by hour, to wander on,
And, as they neared them, turned to wastes of sand.
They thirsted, and with looks of blank despair
Beheld the emptied skins.   One only, borne
By Ka'ab's camel, met their wistful gaze,—
Ka'ab, the rich, the noble, he who knew
The depths of   ,¹ unto Allah's will
Resigning all his soul.   And now he showed
How out of that submission flows the strength

For noblest acts of love.   That priceless store
He claimed not as his own: the 'mine' and
 ' 'thine'
Of selfish right he scattered to the winds,
And to his fellow-pilgrims offered all.
They shared it all alike.   To Ka'ab's self
And Ka'ab's slave an equal portion came :
"Allah is great," he cried, about to drink
With thankful adoration, when a wail
Of eager craving burst from parchèd lips,
And upturned eyes with fevered anguish watched
The precious life-draught.   Ka'ab heard that cry,
His eye beheld that anguish, and his heart
Was stirred with pity.   Tasting not a drop,
With calm and loving look he passed the cup
' To those poor dying lips, and bore his thirst,
As martyrs bear their flames.   His soul had learnt,
Not' Islam's creed alone that God is great :
A mightier name was written on his heart,
"God, the compassionate, the merciful ;"
And yielding up his will to God's, the three,
Compassion, mercy, greatness, were as one.
   So ends the tale.   And whether death came soon
As sleep's twin-brother, with the longed-for rest,
And clear, bright streams in Paradise refreshed
The fevered thirsts of earth ; or if the dawu
Revealed the distant gleam of Mecca's shrine,
And led those pilgrims on to Zemzem's fount.

K

We know not. This we know, that evermore,
Like living water from the flinty rock,
Gladdening the hearts of Hagar's sons, as once
God's angel helped the mother and her child,
The memory of that noble deed flows on,
And quickens into life each fainting heart,
And through long ages, in each Arab's tent
It passed into a proverb—" Ka'ab's deed
Of noble goodness :—There is none like that."³

III.

THE setting sun fell low on Zutphen's plain ;
The fight was over, and the victory won,
And out of all the din and stir of war
They bore the flower of Christian chivalry,
The life-blood gushing out.   He came, the pure,
The true, the stainless, all youth's fiery glow,
All manhood's wisdom, blended into one,
To help the weak against the strong, to drive
The Spaniard from a land which was not his,
And claim the right of all men to be free,
Free in their life, their polity, their faith.
He came, no poor ambition urging on,
But loyalty and duty, first to God,
And then to her, the Virgin Queen, who ruled
His guileless heart, and of a thousand good

Found him the best.   We wonder that he bowed
Before so poor an idol, knowing not
That noble souls transfer their nobleness
To that whereon they gaze, and through the veils
Of custom or of weakness reach the heart
That beats, as theirs, with lofty thoughts and true.
And now that life was ebbing.   Men had hoped
To see in him the saviour of the state
From thickening perils, one in open war
To cope with Alva, and in subtle skill,
Bating no jot of openness and truth,
To baffle all the tortuous wiles of Spain :
And some who knew him better hoped to see
His poet's spirit do a poet's work,
With sweetest music giving voice and shape
To all the wondrous thoughts that stirred the age,
Moving the world's great heart, attracting all,
The children at their play, the old man bent
By blazing hearths, to listen and rejoice.
　　And now his sun was setting.   Faint and weak
They bore him to his tent, and loss of blood
Brought on the burning thirst of wounded men,
And he too craved for water.   Brothers true,
Companions of his purpose and his risk,
Brought from the river in their helmet cup
The draught he longed for.   Yet he drank it not ;
That eye had fallen on another's woe,
That ear was open to another's sigh,

K 2

That hand was free to give, and pitying love,
In that sharp pain of death, had conquered self.
The words were few and simple : " Not for me ;
I may not taste : He needs it more than I : "
Few as all noblest words are, pearls and gems
Of rarest lustre ; but they found their way,
More than all gifts of speech or poet's skill,
To stir the depths of England's heart of hearts,
And gave to Sidney's name a brighter life,
A nobler fame through all the immortal years,
Than Raleigh's friendship, or his own brave deeds,
Or counsels wise, or Spenser's silver notes,—
A trumpet-call to bid the heart awake,
A beacon-light to all the rising youth,
Fit crown of glory to that stainless life,
The perfect pattern of a Christian knight,
The noblest hero of our noblest age.

IV.

AND one day they shall meet before their God,
The Hebrew, and the Moslem, and the flower
Of England's knighthood.   On the great white
        throne
The Judge shall sit, and from his lips shall flow
Divinest words : " Come, friends and brothers,
        come ;

I speak as one whose soul has known your pangs ;
Your weariness and woe were also mine ;
The cry, ' I thirst,' has issued from these lips ;
And I too would not drink, but bore the pain,
Yielding my will to do my Father's work,
And so that work was finished ; so I learnt
The fullest measure of obedience, learnt
The wide, deep love embracing all mankind,
Passing through all the phases of their woe
That I before their God might plead for all.
And thus through all the pulses of their life
I suffer when they suffer , count each deed
Of mercy done to them as done to Me,
Am one with them in sorrow and in joy,
Rejoicing in their likeness to My life,
And bearing still the burden of their sins
For which I once was offered.   I was there,
The Light of each man's soul, in that wild cave,
On that parched desert, on that tented field ;
That self-forgetting love I owned as Mine,
And ye who, true to that diviner Light
Which triumphed over nature, freely gave
That water to the thirsty, gave to Me.
Brother, and friend, and Lord of all men, I
Count nothing human alien from myself,
And lifted up upon the Cross, I draw
By that supremest love the hearts of all.
Come therefore, come, ye blessed, to the Light

That, shining through the world's great darkness, led
Your feet the upward path.   That Light ye saw,
Or dimly dawning on the mountain height,
Or bursting forth in glory as the morn,
Or brightening onward to the perfect day,
And, seeing it, were glad.   Ye heard the Voice
Which bade you mount the steep and narrow way,
And did not close your ears.   Ye knew not then
Whence came the Light, and whose the Voice that
        spake :
Now when all mists are fled, and ever hushed
The world's loud murmur, ye shall see and hear,
As children looking on their Father's face,
And welcomed by their Brother's words of peace.
Yours was the work of yielding all for Him,
Through clouds and darkness pressing on in faith ;
Yours the reward of looking back on life,
The fight well fought, the race well run, to see
That all things true and good were wrought in God."

May, 1864.

'VIE DE JÉSUS.'

(PAR ERNEST RENAN.)

———◦◦———

" HAS then the Christ departed? Is there
                none
To whom the lonely and the lost may turn ?
Does one cold mist of doubt, distrust, despair,
Enwrap the carcase of a sunless world?
The Son of God, the Son of Man, is gone,
Before whose throne we spake adoring praise ;
And through the shadows of the past we see
A graceful Rabbi, dreaming glorious dreams,
Dizzied with fame, then weakly stooping low
To poor deceits, whose death alone redeemed
The clouded life, and saved him from the taint
Of conscious falsehood.   And the lips that speak
These bold revilings once have hymned His praise ;
Those hands have waved the censer's fragrant
                smoke,
Those knees have knelt upon the altar stairs,
That heart has loved the sacred wounds of Christ !

Why falls not fire from Heaven? why opes not earth
The jaws of Hades? And our zeal is cold;
We listen and we argue, when the sword
Were our best answer, cutting down the pride
That dares blaspheme the Lord and Christ we love.
  "But since the days are evil, and men's thoughts
Assert their freedom, other course is ours.
To battle for the faith with arms of proof,
Denouncing, taunting, warning men to shun
The tainted page, to prop the tottering Truth,
Condemning doubts and questions that before
We passed uncensured :—that may help us on
To firmer faith, to high repute of zeal.
Perhaps some fame may follow, and the eyes
Of men admiring watch us as we stand
(As Phinehas stood of old to stay the plague)
Between the dead and living, warding off
Doubt's fell disease, defenders of the faith.
Sweet are those praises to a righteous zeal,
The plaudits of the timid and the good;
And not less sweet the murmurs of the few
Who carp at our advancement. And the praise
May bear its fruit, the title and the wealth, .
The years of manhood in abounding ease,
The age of stately honour. When some years ·
Have passed away, when doubts and answers both
Are clean forgotten, this may yet remain,
For us the only issue of the strife."

The *only* issue ?—What of those long years
That lie beyond the manhood and the age,
The sickness, and the death ?   In that far land,
Throughout the eternal ages, will thy thoughts
Run on thus smoothly ?   Hast thou learnt indeed
To read the times and seasons ?   Hast thou heard
The witness which the doubter bears to thee ?
Thou priest, with waving censer, mitred brow,
And cope all stiff with crimson and with gold,
Hast thou forgotten that the Christ was man ?
Hast thou left vacant all the heart's desire,
And mocked it with the likeness of a child
Or image of the Crucified ?   Thy Lord
Has given thee all the records of His life,
And thou hast made them silent.   Wonder not
That men should fill the gap with aught that brings
The living Man before them.   They *will* have
A Jesus with the pulse of human life,
The throbs of human feeling.   Failing that,
No pageant show will draw them on to faith,
Nor music's spell enchant them, nor the power
Of ancient systems lull their souls asleep :
But give them this,—proclaim the living Christ,
The youth, the man, all tempted, struggling, worn,
Labouring and suffering as the millions now
Suffer and labour, homeless, poor, contemned,
Not clothed in purple, faring daintily,
But sharing peasants' food in peasants' huts ;

And tell them that He bowed Himself to this,
To all the shame, the agony, the Cross,
For them, and sufferers like them,—and be sure
Thou wilt find listeners.   Not the gilded shrine
Of Virgin-Mother, clad in gorgeous robes
All star-bespangled, when the anthem swells,
And incense-fragrance floats through loftiest choir,
Will draw more hearts to worship than the tale
Of One who came their Brother and their Friend,
Sharing their nature, living all their life.

And thou, thou boaster of a purer faith,
Zealous to censure this extreme or that,
Is there no message for thy soul to hear ?
Hast thou made Christ the leader of a sect,
Within thine own poor limits narrowing down
The wider pulses of His human heart ?
Hast thou made much of words, and forms, and tests,
And thought but little of the peace and love,
His Gospel to the poor ?   Dost thou condemn
Thy brother, looking down, in pride of heart,
On each poor wanderer from the folds of Truth ?
Dost thou gloss over as a venial sin
The trespass of the rich, his selfish state,
His pomp, and pride, and luxury, pressing hard,
As did the Pharisees of old, on sins
That others yield to ?   Art thou swift to bind
Thy burdens on the poor, still making sad

The hearts which God would gladden? Hast thou
    turned
To lifeless dogma all the living truth,
Feeding the hungry with the straw and chaff,
Mocking the thirsty with the tainted stream?
Oh! marvel not that they should turn to one
Who tells them of that human heart of Christ,
In spite of all that robs them of their hope,
Their faith in Him who was, and is to come,
The eternal Son of God. Preach thou the Christ,
The Judge of all the mighty ones of earth,
The friend of all the poor and meek of heart,
The foe of all the hypocrites and Scribes,
And thou shalt find thy words wake echoes loud
In hearts of all the multitude who toil,
To whom their Sabbath brings but sensuous rest,
Who enter not or church or chapel gate,
In grim suspicion looking on thy work
As leagued with those against them. Go thy way,
Take Heaven's own armour for the heavenly strife,
Welcome all helpers in thy war with sin;
Make proof, full proof, of all the gifts which God
Has showered upon His Church,—the pastor's care,
The preacher's power, the layman's skill to teach,
His unbought service,—and the end will show
Thou need'st not fear the doubter or his book.
And in thy struggle cease thou not to pray
For him, the poor reviler, who repeats

That ancient blasphemy in accents new,
" He casts out devils by Beelzebub ; "
In wilful blindness he has sinned the sin
Against the Son of Man, yet still he loves
The purity and truth, the grace and peace,
Which drew the hearts of all men.   Pray that still
That love may lead him onward, that the mists
Of that thick-gathering twilight may disperse,
Ere o'er him fall the darkness of the abyss,
The thrice-dread sin which may not be forgiven,
That shuts out love and pity, awe and hope ;
That he, the scorner, low in dust, may lie
Before the bright steps of the Eternal Throne,
And crave forgiveness.   And do thou repent
Of all thy feignèd service of thy Lord,
Of all thy words unreal and thoughts untrue,
And selfish cares, and poor and earth-born fears.
Judge thou thyself, the lost ones seek and save,
And learn through all the future of thy years
To form thy life in likeness of thy Lord's.

May, 1864.

RIZPAH THE DAUGHTER OF AIAH.

I SIT in the silence of evening; the shadows are
   falling apace,
And forms that have vanished flit round me. The
   years that are past I retrace :
The scroll of my life is unrolled ; one moment of vision
   enough
To grasp all the joys and the sorrows, to travel the
   smooth and the rough.
First come the days of my childhood, fair home on
   the Gilead hills,
The cool balm-scent of the breeze, and the music of
   murmuring rills ;
I joyed in the moist green meadows where Jordan
   lovingly flows,
Bright with the golden lilies, and flushed with the
   purple rose ;
The kids of the goats bleated kindly, following me to
   the stream,

And the eyes of the tame gazelle made me glad with
their womanly gleam.

When heroes and chiefs of my tribe marched by with
their shield and their lance,

And forth from the gates of the city came maidens
with song and with dance,

Who but I was foremost among them, ʹrejoicing,
timbrel in hand,

To welcome the men stout of heart who had fought
for our fathers' land?

We mourned not then for the dead : not as the fools
had they died,

But warring against the uncircumcised, taming the
Philistines' pride :

The sword of Jehovah was theirs, the Lord of Sabaoth
their guide.

And then when our bondage was over, we went forth
at eve from the gate

(No fear of the noise of archers), round the wells to
gather and wait,

Drawing water for mothers and children, from well
deep, sparkling, and cool,

Instead of the few scant drops from the city's defilèd
pool.

Ah, bright were the days, and pleasant, the golden
spring of my year;

Now the flowers of the spring are all withered, my life
is wasted and sere.

Full strange was the chance of my life ; I passed from
    a fond mother's side
To be the beloved of a king, in all but name a king's
    bride.
Saul saw me, and loved me, and won me, the king,
    the anointed, the brave ;
Gladly for him had I died, yea, gladly had lived as
    his slave.
Worthy of love he stood, in the stately pride of his
    height,
And towered above Israel's hosts, armed and arrayed
    for the fight ;
That lofty form was the dwelling of soul full as lofty
    and great ;
The soul of a king was there, strong in its love and its
    hate.
And mine, oh ! mine was the love ; the warrior, mighty
    to slay,
In his giant embrace would fold me, with my braided
    tresses would play ;
And ev'n when the dark hour came, and the hand
    of the Lord on him fell,
And instead of the clear light of heaven, brought the
    clouds and the darkness of hell ;
When moody and sullen he sat, and all were afraid
    to draw near,
When David fled from his presence, and Jonathan
    shrank from his spear,

When curses fell thickly around, and the madness all
    soothing defied,
I still might draw near without dread, might safely
    crouch at his side.
If I failed to equal *his* skill, the shepherd-boy with his
    song,
David, fair-faced, golden-haired, his soul as yet guiltless
    of wrong,
Trained by the prophet of Ramah the songs full and
    deep to intone,
Whose music floats, like the incense, upward through
    clouds to the Throne,
Music that he, my king, when it rose in its wave-like
    swell,
From the white-robed band of seers, with a strange,
    o'er-mastering spell,
Silent and rapt, would list to, till he bowed to its
    mighty sway,
And with kingly robes cast off, all night on the hard
    earth lay;
And instead of the curses of madness, instead of the
    silent despair,
Joined in the great Hallelujah that burst, like a storm,
    through the air,
" Is Saul too among the prophets?" men said, in their
    wonder and scorn,
As the deep waters welled from the soul, through the
    might of that music new-born.

This was not mine to do, but my woman's heart had
 the trick
To pour in its Gilead-balm when the iron had pierced
 to the quick ;
My touch on that burning brow would soothe the
 frenzied despair ;
My smile would bend into fondness that fixed and
 terrible glare :
No curses dark, no maddened rage, might my soul
 in its deep love, appal ;
Though God and man might forsake him, he was
 yet mine own, my king Saul.

 Children around us grew : Armoni, the brave and
 the bold,
With bright eyes like an antelope's, and locks of
 burnished gold ;
Mephibosheth, oh, how unlike the crippled slave who
 lives,
And eats at David's table of the bread his master
 gives !
No cripple, my Mephibosheth, but supple, lithe of limb,
Before Jehovah fair and bright, none might compare
 to him.
When the day of his weaning came, hour of a fond
 mother's pride,
Kish came, and Abner, to greet us ; they came from
 the hills far and wide,

The elders of Gilead brought gifts, the corn, and the
oil, and the wine,
Cheese from the milk of the goats, and fruit of the
fig-tree and vine ;
With dancing and song in their joy, in music exulting
and wild,
They sang the praise of my boy, the praise of my
own princely child.

Now all is gone as a dream. The king (though I
saw it not)
Fell fighting with Philistines in the battle fierce and hot.
On Gilboa's heights he fell : God's curses on them
rest !
May no dew of heaven fall on them, be they barren
and unblest !
He fell, his brave son with him ; the uncircumcisèd
crew
In that dark hour my noble Saul, the Lord's anointed,
slew ;
On Bethshan's wall they hung him, all stript and
stained with blood,
The ghastly sport of scoffers, and the vulture's hideous
food ;
The king who had clothed us in purple, the pride of
his people, hung there,
Shaming the sun in the heavens, poisoning the summer
night-air.

Blest be the warriors of Gilead, the men of Jabesh the
    strong ;
They had not forgotten the hero who saved them
    from outrage and wrong ;
By night they came silent and swift ; not plundering,
    eager to slay,
But holy and pure in their souls as the priests when
    they stand up and pray.
They stole to the gate of the city ; the watchmen slept
    on their posts ;
Speechless they crept on the walls, through the
    slumbering Philistines' hosts ;
Goodly the spoil they brought back, the mouldering
    bones of the brave ;
They gave them a chieftain's burial, they dug them a
    chieftain's grave ;
Under that old oak of Jabesh they laid him, the
    lordly, the tall ;
For seven days and nights they wept sore over their
    king, and my king, my Saul.

  It was well. David heard it. It pleased him : he
    too would lament.
Over the beauty of Israel. In every Israelite's tent
That song of the Bow re-echoed,[1] which told of the
    father and son,
Lovely and pleasant together, in life as in death ever
    one ;

Which told of the wonderful love, tender, and fervent,
    and true,
The love of the pure and the stainless, love granted
    only to few.
" Passing the love of woman," he called it.   Well
    might he call ;
He gauged not the depths of my heart, my love for
    my hero, my Saul ;
He married for power or for wealth, paving his steps
    to the throne ;
Men might admire him and love, but no woman's
    heart was his own ;
Michal, Saul's daughter, she scorned him, and Bath-
    sheba's homage, I ween,
Was not as a true maiden's love, but the trick of a
    would-be queen.

The days of my mourning were over.   I wept for
    my dead for a while ;
But a mother needs must rejoice in the light of her
    children's smile :
They grew in their youth, and their manhood, keen-
    eyed, quick of foot and of hand,
And Abner spake loud in their praise, as the first of
    his goodly band.
Abner, the brave, he too loved me ; I was fain to
    love him in return ;
To whom in her desolate shame could the outcast
    concubine turn ?

Yet not as Saul could I love him; the freshness of
    passion was gone,
Which sweeps the whole current of life to its loved
    one exultingly on;
I was fair in his sight; and he, I found him kindly
    and brave;
I was true as a wife to her husband, and wept true
    tears at his grave.
My sons too found him a father: he taught them the
    use of the bow,
Taught them to strike down the lion, to fight, hand
    to hand, with the foe.
They fought for the birthright of Saul in that long
    and lingering strife.
The sons of a king were they, in them flowed the
    kingly life: ·
They were true to their name and their fame, true
    to their oath and their word,
Till at last the struggle was over, and Israel owned
    David as lord.
"Now," I thought, "they are mine till I die. The
    danger is over, is past;
My life will no longer be dreary, the sky is no longer
    o'ercast."

II.

So it was for a time; but ere long there fell upon
  Israel a curse,
Evil still following on evil, bad passing on into
  worse;
No showers fell softly from heaven, the streams of
  the hills were all hushed,
The hot sun had burnt them all up, and the sky as
  a furnace was flushed;
Red, fierce, and malignant its rays, like flames from
  a fathomless hell,
Over the dry, parched vineyards and the desolate olive-
  grounds fell;
Wild asses ran hither and thither, snuffing the air as
  they went,
The streams that water the valleys were long since
  vanished and spent.
Iron-bound and hard was the earth: no tender
  herbage was seen;
No fresh corn gladdened the eyes with its tufts of
  feathery green;
The fair broad valleys of Shechem were like one vast
  desert of sand,
And the people fainted with hunger; the famine was
  sore in the land.

Three years passed over our heads, with the sickness
    of hope deferred ;
They prayed, but they prayed in vain; not a voice
    to answer was heard ;
The king mourned sore for his people, the people
    were hushed in despair :
What arm but their God's could relieve them? and
    that arm against them was bare.
When vision and prophet had failed them, they turned
    in their utter distress
To the great High Priest of our nation, and he, in
    his priestly dress,
In the bright robes of Aaron his father (so have they
    told me the tale)
Entered the Holy of Holies, the darkness within the
    veil ;
The twelve bright gems on his breast, that he for
    his people might plead,
No tribe unremembered there in that hour of the
    nation's need ;
And over his heart there sparkled the Urim's mys-
    terious glow,[2]
Its wild, oracular rays pregnant with weal or with
    woe ;
As he went (so they told me) it gleamed with the
    lurid, terrible red,
Which told that blood-guilt was upon us, that for
    blood more blood must be shed.

And Abiathar standing there, with fixed, immoveable
  gaze,
Looked down through the thick, black darkness on
  the strange, disastrous blaze.
Long time he stood stiffened and dumb, by the hand
  of Jehovah oppressed;
At last, half-choked as he spake it, the hollow voice
  came from his breast:
Forth from his faltering lips the death-bearing oracle
  flew:
" For Saul and his bloody house, for them who the
  Gibeonites slew,
For them has the curse fallen on us, for them has
  the land waxen faint;
Theirs is the putrid sore, yea, theirs is the pestilent taint;
The sword of the Lord will fall heavy alike on evil
  and good;
All have shared in the guilt by their silence—the land
  is defilèd with blood."

I knew it. That slaughter was evil. They had not
  wronged him, those slaves,
Hewing wood, drawing water, nought else, till they
  slept in their graves:
No glory was there to win, no men of renown to
  lay low;
They perished as brute beasts perish, bowing their
  heads to the blow;

Why should Saul, the hero, the strong, stain his sword
    with the blood of the weak ?
What led him on children and women his terrible
    vengeance to wreak ?
I know not. The deed was done. In vain for mercy
    they cried ;
The oath of our fathers availed not ; Saul gave the
    command, and they died.
It was true : I may not deny it ; atonement was
    needed. No time
Could blot out that foul stain of blood, could cancel
    that dark day of crime ;
The cries of the widow and orphan had risen for
    vengeance on high ;.
Thence came the drought and the famine, the curse
    on the earth and the sky ;
Gladly we offered our treasures, our gold and our
    silver, our all,
To build up the desolate homes made empty and
    lonely by Saul.
But, oh ! was it right to risk all on the hated
    Gibeonites' choice,
The lives of the freemen of Israel to hang on the
    bond-slaves' voice,
The sons of a king to perish for obeying their
    father's command,
As the scapegoat dies in the wilderness, bearing the
    sins of the land ?

Wily and subtle as ever, the Gibeonites scoffed at our
    prayer;
No sight would glut their revenge but the looking
    on our despair;
They knew that the fallen are friendless.   One only
    King David would save;
The son of his darling Jonathan might creep to his
    father's grave;
Dearly did Michal pay for the taunt of her passing
    scorn,
When the five who called her mother from her fond
    embrace were torn.
Was it well this deed should be his, the Psalmist-king
    who had told
Of truths that our fathers knew not in the rougher
    days of old?
From the white-robed choir of the Levites, in the
    courts of our Sacred Tent,
His hymns had spread through all Israel, waking new
    thoughts as they went,
Proclaiming to all that no blood of bulls or of goats
    might avail,
That thousands of rams, ten thousands of rivers of
    oil would fail,
That one thing only God asks for, the broken and
    penitent heart,
That all who repent and believe in the glad news of
    mercy have part.

Was it right that *he* should disown this, that human
    victims should bleed,
As for Moloch, the King of Gehenna, to the true
    God of Abraham's seed ?
Was the sickening odour that tainted the soft south
    wind as it passed,
A fragrance of sweet-smelling incense that in His sight
    found favour at last ?

I know not : faint, weary, perplexed, I bowed my
    head to the shame,
I did not tremble or weep when the hour of my
    agony came :
They led them out one by one, they fastened each
    to his cross,
While I, the mother, stood silent, counting my infinite
    loss ;
With nail and with cord they bound them, each one
    to his cursèd tree
On the hill of Gibeah of Saul (so ran King David's
    decree),
Before the Lord they hanged them, with muttered
    curses and prayer,
And the priests laid the sins of the nation on their
    heads of waving hair ;
In Gibeah of Saul, in the home where they in their
    childhood had played,
And their father's heart had exulted, as he sat in the
    terebinth's shade,

In Gibeah of Saul, where of old the people had
    hailed him as king,
Glad to repose for a while, their jubilant praises to
    sing.

A few days before, when as yet the barley was
    green in the ear,
They and I ate our Passover meal. We wept not;
    no tear
Made the bitter herbs yet more bitter.   With solemn,
    unwavering voice
They sang of the stretched-out arm that had made
    our fathers rejoice.
It was over, that feast.   Ere yet the people had
    gone to their home,
Ere the sickle was put to the corn, or the ripening
    wave-sheaf had come,
They led them forth one by one, my own, my goodly
    and brave.
They trembled not, feared not: not with the dread
    of the slave,
Not with the fire of the warrior struggling with
    passionate breath,
Not with the tears of a woman, went they to the
    hour of their death.
Strange peace, not of earth, had come o'er them.
    They stood there, willing to die,
Offered for Israel's sake, to draw rain from the hot,
    sullen sky.

Without one struggle or cry, calm in their patience
    they stood, ·
Calm as when Abraham, our father, laid Isaac, his
    son, on the wood,
Patient as Isaac was when he bowed his head to the
    knife ;
Dumb as the sheep to his shearers, so they, too, yielded
    their life.

That, too, was over.   The crowds were scattered
    each to his own ;
The darkness came over the land.   I was left to
    mourn there alone ;
I looked on the pale, wan features that once I had
    lovingly pressed,
Sweet with the fragrant oil as a field which the Lord
    God hath blest ;
I looked on the tortured forms, which once were
    supple and lithe,
Leaping from crag to crag, as the roebuck joyous
    and blithe ;
Weary and worn I slept not, yet my waking thoughts
    were as dreams ;
Through the dark overhanging shadows there came
    strange and wonderful gleams.
I had asked in my woe, " How came this ?   Why did
    evil begin ?
Why should fresh curse upon curse fall, heaping sin
    upon sin ?

Why was their youth cut off in all its beauty and
    prime?
How could their blood atone for their own or their
    fathers' crime?"
A voice came forth from the darkness, just heard in
    the silence of night,
A whisper making one tremble, a murmur ineffably
    light;
"And hast thou not learnt it, O mourner? hath not
    the oracle come,
Giving sight to the eyes that were blind, giving speech
    to the lips that were dumb?
Thy sons, thou hast loved them of old, but when in
    thy life didst thou know
The power of love in its might till that love was
    mingled with woe?
When were they worthiest of love?   Was it when
    eager and young,
They chased the wild deer on the hills, and, leaping,
    rejoiced as they sung?
Was it when, ardent, exulting, they fought with the
    foes of their race,
To the fiercest and bravest of all turning their lion-
    like face?
Or is it not now, when thou seest them a sacrifice
    meet for the Lord,
Willing victims, self-offered, pure, looking on high for
    reward?

Yes, He owns them, their Father, their God, the
    Almighty, All Good,
Not as Moloch, the King of Gehenna, delighting in
    slaughter and blood,
But rejoicing, accepting, forgiving, whenever the fire
    of his love
Burns in the hearts of his servants, as it burns in
    the seraphs above,
When, ceasing to live for themselves, they are ready
    to die for their race,
Willing as cursèd to suffer, that it may find mercy
    and grace :
Through all the confusions of guilt, David's weakness,
    the Gibeonites' wrong,
Through all the harsh discords and darkness God is
    still eternally strong ;
The thick clouds of evil pass off, the distant horizon
    is clear,
The day-star of hope has arisen, the dawn of Redemp-
    tion is near."

    As the word of the Lord comes to prophet or
    priest, so it came,
Making my bones to tremble, burning my heart with
    its flame,
And then as new thoughts woke within me, I
    questioned once more :
"Ah me, if the death of my sons can thus avail to restore,

Can turn from a sin-stained land the darkness that
     over it hung,
Giving life to the perishing soul, giving speech to the
     faltering tongue,
What might not He do, when He, the King, the
     Anointed shall come,
Claiming us all as His people, leading us all to His
     home ;
He whom our prophets have told of, saying to His
     Father, ' Thy will,
Yea, even thine, O my God, have I come upon earth
     to fulfil.'
If a king were to reign on this earth, not warring
     and slaying, like Saul,
But ruling in mercy and peace, loving and gentle
     to all,
Nobler and truer and kinder than David was in his
     youth,
Walking in stainless purity, clad in invincible
     truth;
If He, in the depth of His love, were willing His
     people to save
From all that torments and divides them, from death
     and the power of the grave ;
If He, as my sons hang before me, were to hang on
     the cursèd tree,
Self-yielding His life when His will to keep or to lose
     it was free,

Choosing to suffer man's sorrows, choosing man's
    burden to bear,
Tempted as they are tempted, tasting their doubt and
    despair,
Would not that life be great beyond all man's fancy
    can dream?
Would not that death be strong in the might of its
    power to redeem?
There also my sorrow, it may be, shall not be con-
    temned in his eyes;
There, also, a mother's fond love may watch by the
    cross till He dies.
I feel I can measure her grief: I dare believe He
    would turn
His pitying look upon me, nor the sin-stained con-
    cubine spurn;
Outcast and scorned though I be, I dream I might
    venture there
To wash His feet with my tears, to wipe those feet
    with my hair."

The vision was over; I woke to my lonely, terrible task,
But hope, strength, life were within me, all I had
    ventured to ask;
On the rock I spread forth my sackcloth, with my
    torch I scared away
The vultures and the dogs unclean that scented out
    their prey.

Day passed on after day, and the harvest-fields grew
    white,
And the maiden-gleaners shuddered as they watched
    the ghastly sight :
All summer long I bore the heat of the fiery sun at
    noon,
And at night I faced the maddening rays of the sullen,
    lurid moon ;
The bodies withered òn the trees, till at last the rain-
    drops fell,
The first fresh showers that blest the earth with soft
    and quickening spell :
" The curse was past," men said, " their fears for the
    future might cease,
The Lord was entreated for Israel ; the land might
    again dwell in peace."

    Men told the king of my watching, and the heart
    of David was moved,
And once again there woke in him the thought of
    those he had loved.
He gave them a kingly tomb : in the grave of their
    fathers they sleep ;
Men may go there to tell of their praise, I may go
    there to sit and to weep :
And the heroes also are there.   In that grave father
    and son,
Lovely and pleasant together, still undivided are one,

My sons, too, sleep with their father, and I, when the
    Angel of Death
Shall summon my soul to depart with the icy cold of
    his breath,
When life's long struggle is over, and the shadows
    over me fall,
Shall lie down to rest by his side, by the side of my
    loved one, my Saul.

March, 1864.

TRANSLATIONS.

I.

THE SONG OF DEBÔRAH.

F OR the day when the chieftains of Israel towered
in the height of their fame,
For the day when the people that followed, self-
offered, with willing hearts came,
Bless ye the Lord in the highest, His might and His
glory proclaim.

Hear, O ye kings of the earth; give ear, ye mighty
and strong;
I, even I, will exalt Him, I will praise Him with
music and song;
To the Lord God of Israel, our king, sing praises to-
day as of old,
When from Seir He came in His glory with wonders
our fathers have told;
From the wild plains of Edom He marched, and the
heavens were shaken with dread;
The torrent-rain fell from the clouds, and the earth
was moved at His tread,

The mountains reeled from their base, they flowed
    as the great deep flows,
And Sinai trembled before Him, when the Lord God
    of Israel arose.

From the old days of Shamgar-ben-Anath, to the
    days of Jael, the land
Lay waste, and devoured by oppressors, a prey to the
    enemy's hand ;
The highways of Israel that echoed the tramp of the
    traveller's tread,
Deserted and silent ran on, as though through the
    realms of the dead ;
The straggler that journeyed alone, in his fear of the
    foeman's wrath,
In the dark shade of evening stole through the wild
    hills' wildest path ;
The villagers ceased to assemble, they cowered from
    the sight of their foes,
Until I, Debôrah, appeared, as a mother in Israel arose.
Then, at length, new chieftains they chose, as Gods
    to guide and to save ;[1]
Once more in their gates was heard the shout of the
    warlike and brave ;
Yet not even then did they meet as an army arrayed
    for the fight,
Though twice ten thousand were there, not a spear or
    shield was in sight.

My whole heart is eager to greet them, the chieftains
    spotless in fame,
The people who, offering their lives, with brave and
    willing hearts came ;
Bless ye the Lord in the highest, His might and His
    glory proclaim.
And ye who ride forth on white asses, as princes and
    counsellors ride,
Ye who sit in the gate to give judgment, let your
    voice be heard by their side ;
From the lips of those who rejoice at eve round the
    wells cool and calm,[2]
Let the right deeds of God swell your hearts with
    the tones of the jubilant psalm,
The right deeds of God, which He for the people of
    Israel hath done,
The people He claims as his own, who went forth to
    the battle, and won.

  Awake, awake, O Debôrah, awake, Oh, awake to the
    song,
Arise, O son of Abinoam, arise, O Barak the strong,
Lead forth thy conquered, thy captives, marching
    in triumph along.[3]

  The battle was won by the few; of our host but a
    remnant was there ;
But that remnant was noble in heart, and the Lord's
    arm to help them was bare ;

Above all the heroes, the strong ones, to me was the
  victory given;
A woman's voice guided that host, her words were as
  counsels from Heaven.
Foremost of all, ye came, ye warriors of Ephraim,
  our pride,
True stock of the heroes of old who fighting with
  Amalek died;⁴
After you came the bravest of Benjamin, goodly and tall;
From Machir the chiefs of Manasseh rushed down
  to the fight at my call;
Zebulun sent forth her sons; with the sceptre of
  princes they came;
And Issachar also was true to the height of his
  ancient fame;
By the side of Debôrah the princes of Issachar fought
  as she led,
By the side of Barak they marched down the valley
  with conquering tread.

  Behold! by the fair streams of Reuben his chieftains met in debate;
Mighty the stirrings of counsel, the searchings of
  heart, oh, how great!
Why after all did'st thou linger, tarrying behind in the
  fold,
To list to the bleating of sheep, when the war-cry
  summoned the bold?

By the fair streams of Reuben they gathered, her
   chieftains met in debate,
Mighty the stirrings of counsel, the searchings of heart,
   oh, how great !
And Gilead too held back his strength, content
   beyond Jordan to stay,
And Dan watched the fishermen's boats as they plied
   to and fro in the bay,
And Asher looked out on the waves, and lazily dwelt
   on his coasts ;
Not a man of them all came forth to the help of the
   Lord God of Hosts.
The people who perilled their lives from Zebulun and
   Naphtali came ;
On the heights of the mountains they triumphed,
   fighting for freedom and fame.

   They fought, those kings of the nations, the chiefs
      of the Canaanites' land,
Where the torrent-streams of Megiddo roll down by
   Taanach's strand ;
But not for them was the glory of victors dividing the spoil,
No heaped-up treasure of silver paid them for their
   blood and their toil :
A mightier army than theirs was fighting unseen on
   our side ;
The stars as they moved in their courses made war
   upon Sisera's pride :

The white-foaming waters of Kishon swept them away
in its might,
Kishon, the onward-rushing, swoln with the storm of
the night ;[5]
Struggling, and plunging, and whirling, maddened with
fear and dismay,
The horse and his rider went down ; the proud river
swept them away.

" Curse ye the people of Meroz,"—the word from the
Prophet's lips came,[6]
Whose voice, as an Angel of God's, was mighty to
praise and to blame ;
" Yea, with a bitter curse curse them, the craven,
the faint-hearted crew ;
They came not forth in that hour to the help of God's
chosen and true ;
They left them to struggle alone, the mighty and strong
to pursue."
But blessed, thrice blessed be Jael ; from the tents of
that stranger-band,
The name of the wife of Heber shall sound through
the breadth of the land.
He came, hot and parched to her door, the fever of
battle was strong ;
He asked her for water to drink, for the way was
weary and long ;

With kind words she welcomed him in, and the milk
cool and freshening she poured;
In her costliest vessel she brought it, as a handmaid
waits on her lord.
Weary and faint he slumbered. She put forth her
hand to the nail,
With the workman's hammer she smote it (not then
did her woman's heart quail)—
She smote him there as he lay, through brow and
through temples it went;
Stricken and bleeding, the carcase of Sisera lay in
her tent:
One struggle, one cry; it was over; the hero, the
Canaanites' pride,
At her feet lay lifeless and pale; he bowed, he fell
down, and he died.

Far off in the palace of Jabin, with looks proud,
eager, amazed,
Forth from her latticed window the mother of Sisera
gazed:
"Why lingers the conqueror's chariot? Why hear I
not, borne on the wind,
The clang of the strong iron wheels, and the tramp of
the army behind?"
"Oh! dream not of failure," they answered, her
maidens, swift to divine,

(Yea, like answer she made to herself), "the glory of
    conquest is thine;
Surely they conquer once more.   In triumph they
    bring back their prey;
The maidens of Israel shall yield to the might of their
    captors to-day;
And for Sisera's neck, as he rides in his glory home
    from the fight,
The costliest robes of their priests,' with mingled hues
    glorious and bright,
Broidered by fair maidens' fingers, on both sides
    radiant alike,
Meet for the necks of the heroes whose right hands
    have known how to strike."

  So let them boast in their folly; so let them dream
    in their pride;
So perish thy foes, O Jehovah, dying as Sisera died;
But the people that love Thee, Thy chosen, the heroes
    who walk in Thy light,
Let them shine evermore as the sun when he rides
    through the heavens in his might.

March, 1864.

THE EARLIEST CHRISTIAN HYMN.

(FROM THE GREEK OF CLEMENT OF ALEXANDRIA.)[1]

——•◦•——

CURB for the stubborn steed,
   Making its will give heed ;
Wing that directest right
The wild bird's wandering flight ;
Helm for the ships that keep
Their pathway o'er the deep ;
Shepherd of sheep that own
Their Master on the throne,
Stir up Thy children meek
With guileless lips to speak,
In hymn and song, Thy praise,
Guide of their infant ways.
O King of Saints, O Lord,
Mighty, all-conquering Word ;
Son of the highest God
Wielding His Wisdom's rod ;

Our stay when cares annoy,
Giver of endless joy ;
Of all our mortal race
Saviour, of boundless grace,
           O Jesus, hear.
Shepherd and Sower Thou,
Now helm, and bridle now ;
Wing for the heavenward flight
Of flock all pure and bright ;
Fisher of men, the blest,
Out of the world's unrest,
Out of Sin's troubled sea
Taking us, Lord, to Thee ;
Out of the waves of strife
With bait of blissful life,
With choicest fish, good store,
Drawing Thy nets to shore.
Lead us, O Shepherd true,
Thy mystic sheep, we sue,
Lead us, O Holy Lord,
Who from Thy sons dost ward,
With all-prevailing charm,
Peril, and curse, and harm ;
O path where Christ has trod,
O Way that leads to God,
O Word, abiding aye,
O endless Light on high,

Mercy's fresh-springing flood,
Worker of all things good,
O glorious Life of all
That on their Maker call,
   Christ Jesus, hear.
O Milk of Heaven, that prest
From full, o'erflowing breast
Of her, the mystic Bride,
Thy Wisdom hath supplied ;
Thine infant children seek,
With baby lips, all weak,
Filled with the Spirit's dew
From that dear bosom true,
Thy praises pure to sing,
Hymns meet for Thee, our King,
   For Thee, the Christ ;
Our holy tribute this,
For wisdom, life, and bliss,
Singing in chorus meet,
Singing in concert sweet,
   The Almighty Son :
We, heirs of peace unpriced,
We, who are born in Christ,
A people pure from stain,
Praise we our God again,
   Lord of our Peace.

March, 1864.

HYMNS

FOR

SCHOOL OR COLLEGE,

ETC.

HYMNS FOR SCHOOL OR COLLEGE.

I.

" This is none other but the house of God."

O GOD, whose angels once did bless
    The wanderer in his lonely sleep,
Descending, rising, to and fro,
    Their watch around his couch to keep ;
Be with us now, let seraph tongues
    Breathe forth their song of sin forgiven,
And tell us this is holy ground,
    The House of God, the gate of Heaven.

O Lord, whose glory once did shine
    With mystic cloud the courts to fill,
Which David's Son, in kingly state,
    Had reared on Zion's holy hill :
Be with us now, as Priest and King,
    In clouds and darkness claim thine own ;
Let this our Temple see Thy light,
    Thou Christ upon Thy Father's throne.

O Holy Spirit, Lord of Life,
   Whose voice we hear in varying tones,
Revealing glories yet to come,
   The Temple built of living stones ;
Cleanse Thou our hearts, our roughness smooth,
   And bring us daily nearer Thee,
Within Thine own eternal house,
   As polished corner-stones to be.

O Mystic Three, O Holiest One,
   Thou Lord of Wisdom, Light, and Love,
Give strength to do Thy work on earth,
   Give grace to sing Thy praise above ;
Let infant lips Thy glory speak,
   On youth Thy choicest blessings send ;
Let manhood find its rest in Thee,
   And age grow riper for the end.

So on through all the circling years,
   May reverent footsteps mark the days,
And full-toned voices offer here
   Their morning sacrifice of praise :
So guide us through earth's toilsome paths,
   And bid us onward, upward rise,
That we, when all our work is done,
   May rest with Thee in Paradise.

May, 1864.

II.

"Beholding as in a glass the glory of the Lord."

O LORD of Hosts, all heaven possessing,
　　Behold us from thy sapphire throne,
In doubt and darkness dimly guessing,
　We might Thy glory half have known;
But Thou in Christ hast made us Thine,
And on us all Thy beauties shine.

Illumine all, disciples, teachers,
　　Thy Law's deep wonders to unfold;
With rev'rent hand let Wisdom's preachers
　　Bring forth their treasures new and old;
Let oldest, youngest, find in Thee,
Of Truth and Love the boundless sea.

Let Faith still light the lamp of Science,
　　And Knowledge pass from truth to truth,
And Wisdom, in her full reliance,
　　Renew the primal awe of youth;
So holier, wiser, may we grow,
As Time's swift currents onward flow.

Grant, Lord, that we, in patience gleaning,
　　Thy truths in memory's shrine may store ;
Reveal to us each secret meaning
　　Of all Thy word's divinest lore ;
When round us mists of evening rise,
Shine Thou upon our wistful eyes.

Bind Thou our life in fullest union
　　With all thy saints from sin set free ;
Uphold us in that blest communion
　　Of all thy saints on earth with Thee ;
Keep Thou our souls, or here, or there,
In mightiest love that casts out fear.

May, 1864.

III.

"I am the Way, the Truth, and the Life."

O LIGHT, whose beams illumine all,
   From twilight dawn to perfect day,
Shine Thou before the shadows fall,
   That lead our wandering feet astray ;
At morn and eve Thy radiance pour,
That youth may love and age adore.

O Way, through whom our souls draw near
   To yon eternal Home of Peace,
Where perfect love shall cast out fear,
   And earth's vain toil and wandering cease ;
In strength or weakness may we see
Our heavenward path, O Lord, through Thee.

O Truth, before whose shrine we bow,
   Thou priceless pearl for all who seek,
To thee our earliest strength we vow,
   Thy love will bless the pure and meek ;
When dreams or mists beguile our sight
Turn Thou our darkness into light.

O Life, the well that ever flows
    To slake the thirst of those that faint,
Thy power to bless what seraph knows?
    Thy joy supreme what words can paint?
In earth's last hour of fleeting breath,
Be Thou our conqueror over Death.

O Light, O Way, O Truth, O Life,
    O Jesus, born mankind to save,
Give Thou Thy peace in deadliest strife,
    Shed Thou Thy calm on stormiest wave ;
Be Thou our hope, our joy, our dread,
Lord of the Living and the Dead.

O mightiest Three, O holiest One,
    Of all in heaven and earth the King,
All power and glory Thou hast won,
    To Thee all saints and angels sing ;
Still serving, through the eternal rest,
They do Thy bidding, and are blest.

May, 1864.

IV.

"One generation shall praise Thy works unto another."

O PRAISE the Lord our God,
  In clouds and darkness dwelling,
Yet Fount of shadeless Light,
  All light of earth excelling.
He guides us on to age
  Through sunlit paths of youth ;
He glads our longing eyes
  With full, unveilèd truth.

That truth, O Lord, we seek,
  In spirit meek and lowly ;
To all who learn or teach
  Give wisdom pure and holy.
In solemn awe we bend,
  All wondering, round Thy throne,
And Thee, our Lord, our Life,
  Our Joy, our Gladness own.

O Lord of Truth and Light,
  All heaven and earth possessing,
Grant us Thy laws to know,
  Our daily task-work blessing ;
Teach us Thy love to see,
  O'er earth and heaven outspread,
While Wisdom, conquering Fear,
  With highest Faith shall wed.

All praise and thanks to Thee,
  Eternal Lord, be given,
For all Thy help on earth,
  For all our hopes of Heaven ;
Thy Name, the One, the Three,
  Through æons yet to come,
All saints and angels sing,
  Their Light, their Peace, their Home.

May, 1864.

V.

"I have the keys of Hell and of Death."

O LORD, Thine other names are sweet,
  As music to the listening ear;
But this thrills all our awe-struck heart
  With fitful pulse of gloomiest fear;
Thou King of Heaven—and dost Thou dwell,
The holder of the keys of Hell?

O Light of Love! O Fount of Life!
  Clear spring of joy for all on earth,
Still quickening all to higher mood,
  Thou worker of the second birth;
From Thee we draw each moment's breath,
And art Thou then the Lord of Death?

Yea, Lord! through all that drear abyss,
  Where spirits wail their evil past,
Thy Love and Pity still look on,
  Long-suffering, conquering at the last;
From Thee flow mercy, pardon, peace,
From Thee the woe that shall not cease.

O Christ, Eternal Light of Love!
O Judge, Eternal Fire of Wrath!
Guide Thou our steps the narrow way,
   Oh, lead us on the upward path;
Our darkness let Thy light illume,
Thy fire our baser dross consume.

We need not turn for help or grace,
   To saint's or martyr's pitying ruth,
For Thou art still the Way, the Life,
   In Thee all Mercy meets all Truth;
Oh, leave us not, Thou Lord of All,
Through pains of death from Thee to fall.

Oh, plunge us in Thy priceless blood,
   Oh, purge us in Thy cleansing fire;
Wash out each stain of sinful birth,
   Burn out each taint of low desire;
Through fire and water lead Thine own
To rest before Thy Father's throne.

June, 1864.

PROCESSIONAL.

—◦◦—

"In the name of our God we will set up our banners."

R EJOICE ye pure in heart,
    Rejoice, give thanks, and sing ;
Your orient banners wave on high,
    The cross of Christ your King.

Bright youth and snow-crowned age,
    Strong men and maidens meek,
Raise high your free, exulting song,
    God's wondrous praise to speak.

Yes, onward, onward still,
    With hymn, and chant, and song,
Through gate, and porch, and columned aisle
    The hallowed pathways throng.

With ordered feet pass on ;
    Bid thoughts of evil cease,
Ye may not bring the strife of tongues
    Within the Home of Peace.

With all the angel choirs,
  With all the saints on earth,
Pour out the strains of joy and bliss,
  True rapture, noblest mirth.

Your clear Hosannas raise,
  And Hallelujahs loud,
Whilst answering echoes upward float,
  Like wreaths of incense cloud.

With voice as full and strong
  As ocean's surging praise,
Send forth the hymns our fathers loved,
  The psalms of ancient days.

Yes, on through life's long path,
  Still chanting as ye go,
From youth to age, by night and day,
  In gladness and in woe.

Still lift your standard high,
  Still march in firm array;
As warriors through the darkness toil
  Till dawns the golden day.

At last the march shall end,
  The wearied ones shall rest;
The pilgrims find their Father's home,
  Jerusalem the Blest.

Then on, ye pure in heart,
   Rejoice, give thanks, and sing :
Your orient banner wave on high,
   The cross of Christ your King.

Praise Him who reigns on high,
   The Lord whom we adore ;
The Father, Son, and Holy Ghost,
   One God for evermore.

May, 1865.

ANNIVERSARIES.

"This shall be a Holy Convocation unto you."

ONCE more we meet, the days come round,
   They move in ordered measure,
And summer suns fling all around
   Rich beauty, choicest treasure :
Once more we meet and thank the Lord
For all the mercies on us poured,
   True work and stainless pleasure.

We will not weary, night and day,
   Our Master's taskwork doing ;
Our lips shall tell Thy love alway,
   Men's hearts to answer wooing ;
By Thee in labour or in rest
May spirit, heart, and soul be blest,
   The upward path pursuing.

Thou, Lord, didst love for children weak
   To utter words of blessing,
And those who came with will to seek,
   Went back in full possessing ;
And dear to Thee the voice of youth,
Unstained and walking in the Truth,
   Thy grace and might confessing.

Yea, Lord, Thou giv'st the power to praise,
   Our lips and hearts unsealing,
Our poor and earth-bound souls dost raise,
   Thy glorious work revealing :
Our spirits taught by Thee can rise
To height of angels' harmonies,
   And glow with angels' feeling.

Do Thou then help us to abound,
   Of all good gifts the Giver ;
Against the foes that hem us round
   Send arrows from Thy quiver ;
Through rest and labour, weal or woe,
Let the heart's stream of rapture flow,
   Like full and mighty river.

Then not in vain to life's last breath
   Shall we in faith have striven ;
Glad sounds shall break the hush of death,
   And tell of sins forgiven ;
And we the threefold Name shall praise,
And there before the throne upraise
   The anthems clear of heaven.

June, 1866.

HARVEST.

" He maketh peace in thy borders, and filleth thee with the finest of the wheat."

LO, the weeks come once more ;
　　They bring their golden store ;
The quickening sunbeams flood the world with light ;
　　High in the evening skies,
　　Gladdening our wistful eyes,
Behold the moon of harvest, calmly bright.

O Lord of heaven and earth,
　　Giver of joy and mirth,
Open our lips to shew Thy wondrous praise ;
　　Feeble our hearts and cold,
　　We leave Thy Love untold ;
Oh, give us strength our joyous hymns to raise.

Whether we sow or reap,
　　Whether we toil or sleep,
Thou givest life and joy, and Thou alone ;
　　Grant Thou to each and all,
　　That, when the shadows fall,
We stand, true servants, round our Master's throne.

So our life's taskwork o'er,
Set free for evermore,
,'e shall sit down at Thy great harvest feast ;
Reaper and sower met,
The sultry heat forget,
And taste God's love, the greatest as the least.

Nay, Lord, Thou too dost claim
The sower's mystic name,
Thou sendest forth Thy reapers to their task ;
Bless them that they may bear
The full corn in the ear ;
Give in Thy bounty more than all we ask.

Root out the evil tares,
Earth's vexing griefs and cares,
Bind the hot blasts that wither and destroy ;
And when the time is come
To bring the full sheaves home,
Bid men and angels share Thy harvest joy.

February, 1867.

HOSPITALS.

"Himself took our infirmities and bare our sicknesses."

THINE arm, O Lord, in days of old,
 Was strong to heal and save;
It triumphed o'er disease and death,
 O'er darkness and the grave;
To Thee they went, the blind, the dumb,
 The palsied and the lame;
The leper with his tainted life,
 The sick with fevered frame.

And lo! Thy touch brought life and health,
 Gave speech, and strength, and sight;
And youth renewed and frenzy calmed
 Owned Thee, the Lord of Light;
And now, O Lord, be near to bless,
 Almighty as of yore,
In crowded street, by restless couch,
 As by Gennesareth's shore.

Though love and might no longer heal
  By touch, or word, or look,
Though they who do Thy work must read
  Thy laws in Nature's book,
Yet come to heal the sick man's soul,
  Come, cleanse the leprous taint ;
Give joy and peace where all is strife,
  And strength where all is faint.

Be Thou our great Deliverer still,
  Thou Lord of life and death ;
Restore and quicken, soothe and bless,
  With Thine almighty breath ;
To hands that work and eyes that see,
  Give wisdom's heavenly lore,
That whole and sick, and weak and strong,
  May praise Thee evermore.
                              AMEN.

June, 1867.

NOTES.

——◦◦——

LAZARUS.

I.

Note 1, p. 3.

——*" And coming there, he asked
For one named Eleazar."*

The name Lazarus is the later Hellenised form of the old Hebrew Eleazar. Between the two we have the transition stage of Eleazarus. As the three forms appear to have co-existed, and to be interchangeable (1 Macc. viii. 17 ; 2 Macc. vi. 18 ; Josephus, *Wars of the Jews*, v. 13, p. 7), I have thought myself free to use both, as occasion might require, though not altogether at random.

In placing the old age of Lazarus and his sisters at Marseilles, I have followed a tradition of considerable antiquity, which the English reader will find in Alban Butler's *Lives of the Saints*, St. Mary Magdalene (July 22), and St. Martha (July 29). Out of this tradition grew (1) the special reverence which the French nation has always shown for the *Madeleine*, whom the popular belief of the Western Church identified with the sister of Lazarus ; and (2) the foundation of a Priory of *Saint Lazare* as the chief church in Marseilles, which gave the name of Lazarists to the devoted followers of Saint Vincent de Paul. (Butler's *Lives of the Saints*, July 19.)

Such a tradition has, of course, no historical authority, yet there is nothing startling or improbable in it. The position of Lazarus, as one whose life was in danger (John xii. 10), would naturally lead to his departure from Jerusalem ; and the intercourse, first between that city and the great commercial cities of Asia Minor, and then between these and Marseilles, was so constant, that that would be as natural a route as any. In the time of Pothinus and Irenæus even, the Gallican Church (French would, of course, be a misnomer) was essentially Asiatic.

Note 2, p. 5.

" Jochanan, once of green Bethsaida's hills."

Here, again, I have thought myself free to use the statelier Hebrew form of the name of the Evangelist instead of the Greek Ioannes, or our own clipt and monosyllabic John. A little later on I have used the same license in substituting Miriam for Mary. A special bond of friendship between the son of Zebedee and the family of Bethany is apparent on the surface of the history. He alone gives the narrative of Lazarus's resurrection. He alone, himself the "disciple whom Jesus loved," tells us that his Master "loved" also "Martha and her sister, and Lazarus" (John xi. 5). The minute detail of narrative in chaps. xi. and xii. is obviously that not of an eye-witness only, but of a friend, for whom every minutest touch—Mary rising hastily, as if going to her brother's grave (xi. 31), Lazarus sitting at the table (xii. 2), the house filled with the odour of the ointment (xii. 3)—had a special and personal interest.

Note 3, p. 8.

———*" and gave me o'er,*
To Polycarp, the shepherd of our flock."

Many readers will have already recognised that I have ventured on reproducing the beautiful story, given " as no myth or legend, but in very deed a history," by Clement of Alexandria. (*Quis dives*, c. 42.) The Bishop is not named by Clement, but the conjecture that it was Polycarp of Smyrna is in itself probable enough, and has met with a fair measure of acceptance. (J. C. Means, in Smith's *Dictionary of Greek and Roman Biography*, art. "Polycarp.")

Note 4, p. 14.

————"*bowed*
Yet more before my wealth."

The fact that the family of Bethany took its position among the richer and more honourable class of the inhabitants, though not expressly stated, is yet distinctly demonstrable.

(1.) Martha is cumbered about "much serving," the cares of a large household (Luke x. 40); and the house is "her own" (x. 38), even though she has a brother living.

(2.) On the death of Lazarus, the Jews—*i. e.*, as St. John always uses the word, the men of mark and influence in Judæa — came out to visit, not the two sisters only, but the kindred who had gathered round them. (John xi. 19.)

(3.) The place of burial was a cave, natural, or hewn out of the rock, like the sepulchre of Joseph, the "rich man" of Arimathea (Matt. xxvii. 57), not a common burying-place.

(4.) The possession of the "pound of ointment of spikenard very costly," priced at more than three hundred *denarii* (John xii. 5), the whole year's wages of a labouring man (Matt. xx. 2), implies that the luxuries and usages of the rich were familiar. The complaint of Judas, that "it *might have been sold*" for that sum, and given to the poor, shows that it was not bought for the special purpose to which it was applied, but formed part of the household stores.

Where facts, and the inferences from them, are so clear, it is hardly necessary to give authorities. I will refer the reader who may wish for them to Archbishop Trench, *On the Miracles*, c. 29.

Note 5, p. 18.

> "*I, Lazarus, the rich,*
> *The ruler, bowing at His feet who came*
> *From Nazareth, the carpenter.*"

The identification of Lazarus of Bethany with the "young ruler" who "had great possessions," which is the turning point of the whole poem, may seem to many very strange and startling. There is no traditional authority for it. I am not aware that any commentator has conjectured it. It must stand or fall on its own evidence. That evidence I submit to the judgment of the reader, in the belief that, though entirely circumstantial and indirect, it yet mounts up to a very high degree of probability; that it rests, to say the least, on infinitely stronger grounds than the current popular identification of Mary Magdalene with "the woman that was a sinner" (Luke vii. 37), or the wide-spread mediæval belief, that both were one and the same with Mary of Bethany; or the conjecture of many commentators, that the "young man with the linen cloth cast about his naked body," who appeared in the garden of Gethsemane (Mark xiv. 51), was St. Mark.

(1.) The total absence of all mention of Lazarus in the first three Gospels is obviously a difficulty which may perhaps be explained, but which we cannot possibly ignore. But a further comparison of the narratives of two of those Gospels with St. John's, presents another like difficulty with regard to the sister of Lazarus. They omit her name entirely, while they record fully the very act which St. John narrates of her (Matt. xxvi. 6 ; Mark xiv. 3 ; John xii. 3), and *must* have known who she was. By them, however, she is mentioned only as "a certain woman." It is a legitimate inference that there was the same reason for silence in both cases.

(2.) But the comparison suggests another question : If the sister was not named, but *the* important act of her life mentioned anonymously, might not the same mode of treatment have been adopted by the same Evangelists as to the brother ? Is it not, at any rate, a natural inquiry to ask, whether there is any unnamed character in their narratives corresponding, in any marked way, to the Lazarus of St. John.

(3.) The next step is to indicate the points of correspondence between the two whom I have ventured to identify.

(1.) The young man is "very rich," "has great possessions," and the wealth of Lazarus has been already proved.

(2.) He is a "ruler," a member, *i. e.*, of the ruling class, probably of the Sanhedrim itself. We are not told this of Lazarus ; but, as has been said, those who came to comfort his sister were of that order, and they came as to an equal. Among those who believed in consequence of the raising of Lazarus were "many among the chief rulers." (John xi. 45 ; xii. 42.) We can hardly doubt that Joseph of Arimathea was one of them, and he was "an honourable counsellor." (Mark xv. 43.) So Nicodemus, also, a "ruler of the Jews" (John iii. 2), takes part in the debates of the Sanhedrim (John vii. 50), and speaks to Jesus, as the young questioner speaks, as to a Rabbi. All this is, at least, presumptive evidence that Lazarus himself, also, was one of the same body. The name Eleazar, we may add, was predominantly a priestly name.

(3.) He is "young," and this agrees with the fact that in John xi. 5, the brother is named after the two sisters, that in Luke x. 38 he is not named at all and the house spoken of as Martha's ; and that in John xii. 2 he is not the giver of the feast at which his sister waits, but is present as a guest.

(4.) He speaks to Jesus as "Master," *i. e.* as Rabbi, and that is the received title which Mary and Martha give to Him in speaking to each other (John xi. 28).

(5.) The question "What good thing shall I do that I may inherit eternal life ?" implies that of the two great Jewish sects, the questioner belonged to that of the Pharisees, and this also is the belief of Martha (John xi. 24). In both also there is the same misconception of that "eternal life," as something in the remote future. The very question with

which he comes is precisely that which would grow out of
our Lord's words to Martha, as to the "good part" which
Mary had chosen.   The brother, seeing in that "*good* part"
something to be done, some act of conspicuous devotion,
might naturally come with the inquiry, " What *good* thing
shall I do ?"

(6.) The spiritual condition of the young ruler and of
Martha is precisely the same.   Each is hindered by the cares
of wealth : to each the same lesson is given in almost the
same words.   To him, "One thing thou lackest" (Mark
x. 21) ; to her, " One thing is needful" (Luke x. 42).

(7.) St. Mark writing, according to the general belief of
the early Church and of many modern critics, from the lips
of St. Peter, records what may well cause our wonder, that
immediately after what sounds like a self-righteous boast,
" ' All these have I observed from my youth ;' Jesus, beholding him, loved him" (x. 20).   That word, used so seldom
of the human affection of our Lord towards individual disciples, limited even among the Twelve to St. John, is used
by St. John himself, the constant companion of St. Peter,
of the family of Bethany, "Jesus *loved* Martha, and her
sister, and Lazarus" (xi. 5).   Martha herself reminds Him
of His love (xi. 3).

(8.) Sad as the conclusion of the young ruler's contact
with the Truth may seem to be, there are even then some
gleams of hope.   We cannot believe that one whom Jesus
"loved" would be left to perish without a prayer, or that
that prayer would not be answered.   The words, " With
God all things are possible," suggest that some process to
free a soul so worthy of love from the evil that was killing it,
would yet be brought to bear on him through the wisdom
and the power of God.   The condemnation of the boastful
pride of the disciples has in it something of the tone of prophecy, " Many that are first shall be last ; and the last first"
(Mark x. 27, 31).   Does not this thought of a great spiritual
miracle to be accomplished through the physical, give the

truest and fullest meaning to our Lord's words on hearing of the illness of Lazarus, "This sickness is not unto death, but for the glory of God, that the Son of God might be glorified thereby" (John xi. 4)? Do not the words, "Father, I thank Thee that Thou hast heard me" (xi. 41), imply a prayer such as the narrative of St. Mark irresistibly suggests?

(9.) The hypothesis of this identity gives, it is believed, a better explanation of the exceptional occurrence of a proper name in the parable of the Rich Man and Lazarus. If we think of the brother of Martha or Mary as being present among the richer Pharisees who were listening, or of them as knowing him well, the choice of the name as indicating that the beggar Lazarus was really more blessed than his namesake, however rich and honoured he might be, receives its full significance. Without this explanation, it is difficult to account for this solitary departure from our Lord's usual mode of teaching.

(10.) On this assumption again, the mention by St. John of one whom the other Gospels had not named has its counterpart in the like treatment of Nicodemus, another "ruler." The part taken by him could hardly have been unknown to them, yet they never name him. They *must* have known who the youug rich ruler (*i. e.*, a member of the great council) was; yet, as of set purpose, they suppress his name; just as they *must* have known the name of the woman in Matt. xxvi. 7, Mark xiv. 3, yet suppress that also.

(11.) The murmur of the disciples and the complaint of Judas in John xii. 4, become more intelligible if we think of . the words, "Sell all that thou hast and give to the poor," as having been spoken to the man who was then among the givers of the feast. "Was not this," they seem to say, "a contravention of an express command?"

The inference from all these data is, I think, all but irresistible, that the first three Evangelists, while deliberately passing over all mention of the name of Lazarus, were yet led to drop hints which were then intelligible to the initiated; and out of which, in combination with the Fourth, it is now possible to construct, approximately at least, a more complete history.   It need hardly be said that, in proportion as this is established, it furnishes the apologist with an answer to objections from their silence against the truth of St. John's narrative.

Note 6, p. 26.

————"*or must I die*
The common death of all men ?"

The tradition is given, but without an authority, by Archbishop Trench, *On the Miracles*, c. 29.

Note 7, p. 28.

———— "*naked, poor,*
Hunted, alone."

I once again venture on a conjecture, not as demonstrable, but as far more probable, including and explaining far more phænomena, than any other.   St. Mark, and he alone (xiv. 51), records the mysterious appearance on the night of the betrayal, and in Gethsemane, of a "young man with a linen cloth cast about his naked body."   The young men, obviously those who had come with the priests and their party, probably young Levites, seize him ; he flies from them, leaving the linen cloth in their hands.   The following points have to be noticed :—

(1.) The age agrees with that of the young ruler and of Lazarus.

(2.) The young man was one who continued to follow Christ in close companionship when all the disciples had already forsaken Him and fled (Mark xiv. 50).   He is as one prepared at last to take up his cross after Him.

(3.) He is one whom the officers of the priests eagerly seize when they allow the escape of the Galilæan disciples, and

Lazarus was the one man about whom such a command had actually been given, whose life·was eagerly sought after (John xii. 9).

(4.) The "linen cloth" (*sindôn*) was one made of the fine linen used by the wealthier class, as in Proverbs xxxi. 24; and noticeably as a winding-sheet in the burial of the rich, as in our Lord's entombment (Mark xv. 46; Matt. xxvii. 59). Such a "*sindôn*" must have been among the grave-clothes so recently used in the burial of Lazarus.

(5.) The nearness of Bethany to Gethsemane falls in with the conjecture. One so apparelled could hardly have come with the soldiers and the priests and officers from Jerusalem. He might well have come over the slope of Olivet to the well-known garden where Jesus resorted ofttimes with his disciples, roused, it may be, by the sudden alarm of the "lanterns, and torches, and weapons," which broke the usually solemn silence of the Paschal night.

LAZARUS.

II.

I have ventured here on the outskirts of a great question,—one which our generation seems called upon to face, and which needs to be faced truthfully and fearlessly. As yet we are living in a warfare of half-truths. Noble and earnest words have been spoken on both sides ; on both sides also, it must be confessed, rash and railing and angry words ; but we look almost in vain on either for even an approximation to a right method of inquiry. Such an inquiry would include a much more careful examination than we have yet had—(1.) Of the varied forms in which the nature and the duration of the punishments of the future life are spoken of in Scripture. (2.) Of the belief on these points then popular and current among the Jews and heathens, and to which, as correcting or confirming it, our Lord's words and those of His apostles, must necessarily have referred. (3.) Of the interpretation given to those words by the earliest Christian thought as shown in creeds and liturgies, prayers for the dead, and nascent purgatorial theories. (4.) Of the rise, progress, and influence, direct and indirect, of the school of Origen. (5.) Of the development of the doctrine of Purgatory in the Eastern and Western Churches. This, however, does but give the exegetical and historical elements of the question. A disciple of Butler, a real seeker after truth, would have to go further and to ask, (6.) What weight is thrown into the scales by the broad facts of human experience ; what analogy, taken by itself, would lead us to expect; (7.) What support it gives, not taken by itself, to the actual teaching of Scripture.

A discussion taking this range is obviously impossible here, and I have given in the poem itself both the phases of thought through which questioners naturally pass, and the conviction in which they may legitimately rest. Unable to accept the bright vision which fascinated the noble heart and intellect of Origen, and was compatible with the higher orthodoxy of Gregory of Nyssa, which in later times was faintly whispered, in one of its forms, by Tillotson and Taylor, and developed with startling boldness by Bishop Newton of Bristol; unable to eliminate from the word "eternal" (I include of course the Greek so rendered) the idea of duration, or in this context to assign to the duration any finite measure; compelled to look upon the punishment of all evil-doers, perhaps of all evil deeds, as in its very nature and by necessary consequence, endless,—I am yet compelled also to look on the popular teaching as to the apportionment and nature of the penalty of sin as miserably defective. It is, I believe, to this defect, to an almost systematic exclusion of the proportion of penalty to sin, to an equally systematic substitution of arbitrary and unrighteous standards of our own for the perfect righteousness which the Judge has himself proclaimed, that we may trace the violent reaction which has led many, not evil livers only, or infidel theorists, but profound thinkers, souls that live in prayer, devoted pastors, to seek to escape from a dogma which seems to them as much at variance, not with their moral sense only, but with Scripture revelations of the character of God, as the Calvinistic theory of reprobation. Truly apprehended, the doctrine of the Church Catholic, as held by the Church of England, presents, I believe, no such antagonism; and those who shrink from the falsehood of extremes and can call no man master, while they learn much from the combatants on either side, may yet find surer guides in the teaching of those who, if they had passions and strifes of their own, are yet removed from ours. From them, from Justin and Clement, the Alexandrian Clement, and Athanasius and Augustine and

Jerome, in the earlier Church ; from Barrow and Butler and
Sherlock and Paley, in our own ; from the more reverential
theologians of Germany, Nitzsch and Stier and Müller—I have
learnt both to accept the words of Scripture in their simplest
and most natural meaning, and to find them in harmony with
the truest thoughts that man forms, with Scripture or without it,
of the righteousness of God.

Note 1, p. 33.

" On fair Pompeii down Vesevus' slope."

The destruction of Pompeii and Herculaneum took place in
A.D. 79, and the impression made by it must have been fresh in
men's minds at the time which I have chosen for the old age of
Lazarus.

Note 2, p. 44.

——— *" One has told, I know,*
Of torments lasting their appointed time."

The questioner might have learnt the hopes or fears that
afterwards expanded slowly into the Romish doctrine of Purgatory from the books that had been to the Greek world as a
witness of the truth of the soul's immortality.   In the beautiful
mythus with which the *Phædon* of Plato ends (p. 113) Socrates
discourses thus :—

" When the dead have reached the place to which each man's
attendant genius (*dæmon*) leads him, first they pass through their
trial, both those who have lived nobly or holily and justly,
and those who have lived otherwise.   And those who appear to
have lived decently go to Acheron, and there, mounting on the
vehicles provided for them, arrive at the [Stygian] lake, and
there they dwell, and being cleansed, and paying the penalty of
their evil deeds, if any one has done evil, are released, and
receive the rewards of their good deeds according to each man's

merit. But those who appear to be incurable, by reason of the greatness of their sins, who have committed many and grievous acts of sacrilege, or many murders foul and unnatural or the like, these their fitting doom casts into Tartarus, and thence they never come forth."

Some, he adds, who have committed great crimes, but "have repented and led a different life," go into Tartarus also, but only for a year.

The old speculation had, however, been recently revived in a form more likely to give it currency.

" Quin et supremo cùm lumine vita reliquit,
Non tamen omne malum miseris, nec funditùs omnes
Corporeæ excedunt pestes ; penitùsque necesse est
Multa diu concreta modis inolescere miris.
Ergò exercentur pœnis, veterumque malorum
Supplicia expendunt.   Aliæ panduntur inanes
Suspensæ ad ventos : aliis sub gurgite vasto
Infectum eluitur scelus, aut exuritur igni.
Quisque suos patimur Manes.   Exinde per amplum
Mittimur Elysium, et pauci læta arva tenemus :
Donec longa dies, perfecto temporis orbe,
Concretam exemit labem, purumque reliquit
Æthereum sensum, atque auraï simplicis ignem."

                                      Virg. *Æn.* vi. 735—747.

The influence of Virgil on the growth of Christian theology, familiar as we are with it in the culminating instance of the *Divina Commedia*, has still, perhaps, to be adequately estimated.

THOUGHTS OF A GALATIAN CONVERT.

Note 1, p. 54.

> " *The beardless priests of Cybele would wave*
> *Their wands, and clash their cymbals.*"

Galatia, like its neighbour Phrygia, was conspicuous for the wild orgiastic worship here described. Atys, after whose example the Galatian priests of the goddess devoted themselves to a life indicated by their beardless faces, was said to have been buried in Pessinus, the chief city of the province, and was worshipped there with festivals and dances, with drums and cymbals and trumpets. Of the frenzy which was thus produced, and the acts to which it led, we have a picture of terrible vividness in the *Atys* of Catullus :—

> "Simul ite, sequimini
> Phrygiam ad domum Cybelles, Phrygia ad nemora Deæ,
> Ubi cymbalûm sonat vox, ubi tympana reboant,
> Tibicen ubi canit Phryx curvo grave calamo,
> Ubi capita Mænades vi jaciunt hederigeræ,
> Ubi sacra sancta acutis ululatibus agitant,
> Ubi suevit illa Divæ volitare vaga cohors ;
> Quo nos decet citatis celerare tripudiis."—19—26.

Such was the religion and the worship in which St. Paul's Galatian converts had grown up, the only religion which they knew till he came among them.

Note 2, p. 62.

"*At eventide,*
When the Jews' Sabbath drew towards its close
(So heard we from our teachers, for no word
Bade us to keep that Sabbath)."

I have assumed, with most students of early Christian ritual, the celebration of the Lord's Supper on the first day of the week, as in Acts xx. 7, and probably 1 Cor. xvi. 2. But then it must be remembered that for those who had been trained, as the framers of that ritual had been, in Jewish modes of reckoning, the evening of Sunday would belong to the second, not the first day; and that the conditions of the case are only met by supposing the celebration to have been fixed for every Saturday, *i. e.*, every Sabbath evening. Starting from this, it is interesting to note that the older customs of the Synagogue presented a point of contact with the new rite. There, also, as the Sabbath closed, bread was eaten, and wine was blessed and drunk in honour of the declining day, as though it were a departing king. (Jost, *Judenthum*, I. p. 180.) Here, also, we have probably the true explanation of the transfer of the ideas of holiness and rest from the seventh to the first day of the week. The Lord's Supper, celebrated first at sunset, then at night, then passing on through midnight to break of day (Acts xx. 7, and Pliny's *Letter to Trajan*), gave its name to the Lord's Day. The adjective, coined especially, it would seem, for the one, was transferred to the other. And the day which had been so begun, men were naturally anxious to honour, as far as their circumstances allowed them, to the end. That the Sabbath, as such, was not enjoined, is obvious from St. Paul's reproof, "Ye observe days, and months, and times, and years" (Gal. iv. 10); "Let no man judge you in respect of an holyday, or of the new moon, or of the Sabbath days." (Col. ii. 16.)

Note 3, p. 63.

" The mighty Maranatha smote the air."

This is not the place to discuss fully the nature of the Pentecostal Gift of Tongues. It is, I believe, demonstrable—(1.) That it did consist in a supernatural power of uttering words and sentences in languages which the speaker was previously unfamiliar with, and which at other times than those in which the power was upon him he could not have spoken at all. (2.) That it was not subject to the control of the understanding, and hardly to that of the will, and therefore was not available, and was, in fact, never used as an instrument of teaching. (3.) That it chiefly showed itself in utterances of ecstatic elevation, raising the worshipper above himself, and so building up his life, though the listeners were not edified, and, if they were strangers, might look on him as mad. As regards the two special points to which I have given prominence here, some evidence may be adduced within the limits which I must prescribe to myself.

(I.) As to the musical character of some, at least, of the utterances of the tongues.

(1.) The analogies which present themselves to St. Paul's mind when he speaks of them are pre-eminently those of musical instruments,—the pipe, the harp, the trumpet (1 Cor. xiv. 7, 8).

(2.) In speaking of their exercise, the instance which first occurs to him is that of "singing in the spirit" (1 Cor. xiv. 15).

(3.) Those who are "filled with the Spirit" (Eph. v. 19), as the disciples had been on the day of Pentecost (Acts ii. 4), are bidden, as their special work, to "sing and make melody in their hearts."

(4.) We can hardly help thinking of other words as referring to the mode of utterance as well as to the words spoken. "By the Spirit," says St. Paul, we *"cry,"* not *say,* "Abba, Father" (Gal. iv. 6; Rom. viii. 15); it "makes intercession for us," when we know not how to conceive and utter our deepest wants, "with *ineffable groanings*" (Rom. viii. 26).

(II.) As to the predominance of Hebrew in the utterance of the tongues as they manifested themselves at Corinth, while I cannot adopt the theory of the greatest Hebrew scholar that the Puritans could boast of in the seventeenth century (Lightfoot, *Harmony of Gospels, on Acts ii.*), that the gift *consisted* in a revival of the true Hebrew of the Old Testament, there seems distinct evidence that it often, and naturally in Greek Churches chiefly, took this form. Thus—

(1.) In the passages referred to, it is the Spirit which leads the worshippers to the utterance of the new cry, so strange to Roman, or Corinthian, or Galatian, of "*Abba*, Father*" (Rom. viii. 15 ; Gal. iv. 6).

(2.) Under a false, counterfeit inspiration, the fearful cry had been in the assembly of the Church of Corinth, "Jesus is Anathema" (1 Cor. xii. 3). When St. Paul, in contrast with this, gives his Anathema (1 Cor. xvi. 22), it is with the addition of the Aramaic word, "Maranatha." The inference is almost irresistible, that that also had been used both in the true and the false utterances.

(3.) The prominence of other Hebrew words, Sabaoth, Hallelujah, Adonai, Hosanna, in Eastern and Western Liturgies, is perhaps traceable to the same source.

Note 4, p. 64.

" converse grave
As though the Lord were listening."

The reader will remember Tertullian's words : "Ita fabulantur ut qui sciant Dominum audire."—*Apologia*, c. 39.

Note 5, p. 68.

"*To Abraham and his seed, that seed being Christ,
(No Mediator there)*."

It has been said, perhaps with some exaggeration, that there
are 430 different interpretations of the words of St. Paul, Gal.
iii. 19, 20. It will not be expected that I should examine them
here.

What seems to be the result of all attempts is this,—

(1.) That St. Paul, when he wrote to the Galatians, was not
thinking or speaking, perhaps had not then learnt to think or
speak, of Christ as a Mediator, and did see one in Moses.
From the point of view of this Epistle, the promise was made
with no mediatorial interposition to Christ Himself as the seed
of Abraham, and to His people *as identified* with Him (comp.
iii. 16 and 29).

(2.) That any mediation did *pro tanto* interpose another
object between the direct intuition of the soul and the unity of
God. The same thought appears in 1 Cor. xv. 28. It is when
the mediatorial work is finished, and the office, as it were, sur-
rendered, that God will once more be "all in all," $\tau\grave{\alpha}$ $\pi\acute{\alpha}\nu\tau\alpha$ $\grave{\epsilon}\nu$
$\pi\hat{\alpha}\sigma\iota\nu$. Rejecting all that was false in the Pantheistic system,
which denied the personality and the holiness of God, there was
yet a Christian Pantheism from which, here and in his address
to the Athenians (Acts xvii. 28), even the Apostle did not
shrink. Afterwards when, from another point of view, he spoke
of "the man Christ Jesus" as the "one mediator between God
and man," it was with a special emphatic assertion that that
character, rightly apprehended, did not obscure the truth of the
Divine Unity, "*There is one God*, and one mediator" (1 Tim.
ii. 5).

In the lines that follow I have endeavoured to bring out the
true meaning of the illustration in Gal. iii. 24. The total ob-
scuration of that meaning by the unhappy, yet perhaps inevitable,
choice of "*schoolmaster*" as the rendering for $\pi\alpha\iota\delta\alpha\gamma\omega\gamma\grave{o}s$, seemed
to make such an attempt desirable.

Note 6, p. 69.

——*"holding rank with those*
Who serve the Goddess-mother at her shrines."

It will be seen that I have adopted what most critics of
repute * receive as the true rendering of Gal. v. 12, and have
followed Dr. Wordsworth's masterly and most interesting note
in pointing out the connexion between the rough, sarcastic word
and the local associations of the Epistle. The Galatians, in
their heathen state, had been accustomed to one form, and one
form only, of consecration to the priesthood of their goddess.
St. Paul's charge against the Judaising preachers of circumcision
is, that they are enslaving his converts to "elements" as "weak
and beggarly" as their old superstition had been (iv. 9). Was it
not natural that he should say, with that thought present to his
mind, that he half wished they would be consistent with themselves, and go back, outwardly as well as inwardly, to the level
of the heathenism which they were practically restoring?

---

* The agreement of Dean Alford, Dr. Wordsworth, and Mr. Jowett, may
fairly be allowed to make up an authoritative *consensus*. Bishop Ellicott is, of
course, a weighty exception.

JESUS BAR-ABBAS.

Note 1, p. 70.

" To build his stately tower by Siloam's pool,
Had seized our sacred Corban,"—

The story of Pilate's wish to make his time of office memo-rable by the construction of an aqueduct to supply Jerusalem with water, of the readiness of the worldly high-priests to allow him to use the treasure, or Corban, of the Temple, and of the frenzy of the people on hearing it, is given by Josephus (*Wars of the Jews*, ii. 9, § 4). The fact may probably be connected with the feeling that the fall of the tower of Siloam was a judgment on the labourers employed in it (Luke xiii. 4). Bar-Abbas, too, we must remember, was more than a common robber. He had been the leader in an insurrection (Mark xv. 7), and it was one that had made him the hero and idol of the people. Chron-ologically the tumult described by Josephus, and the "insur-rection" mentioned by St. Mark, were probably identical.

Note 2, p. 71.

" The creed my Rabbi-father taught my youth."

The name Bar-Abbas, like Bar-jonah, Bar-timæus, was obviously only a patronymic,* and the name, or rather title, of

---

* It was recognised by Anastasius, Bishop of Antioch, as meaning διδασκάλου υἱὸς, the son of a Rabbi.

"Abba, father," was the most coveted among the distinctions which the Rabbis prized (Matt. xxiii. 7). The inference is legitimate enough, and is further interesting as accounting for the eagerness of the Sanhedrim to save the life of Barabbas at the cost of that of Christ.

Note 3, p. 73.

———"*I said my creed,—*
'*Hear, Israel, hear, the Lord thy God is One.*'"

The words of Deut. vi. 4, known from the Hebrew verb with which they open as the Shemà, were looked on as the Israelite's passport to Paradise. It was against the blind confidence that the repetition of the monotheistic formula which they embodied could ensure salvation, and not against any development of St. Paul's teaching that man is justified by faith, that St. James entered his protest, "Thou believest that there is One God ; thou doest well : the *demons* also " (the unclean spirits, who acknowledged the power of that name when exorcised by it) "believe and tremble" (James ii. 19).

Note 4, p. 75.

"*That Galilean prisoner-king, and I,*
Jesus Bar-Abbas."

This form of the name is known to have existed in MSS. earlier than any which are now extant, which were old in the time of Anastasius, Bishop of Antioch, circ. A.D. 560, and is mentioned by Origen. Existing documentary evidence is, it must be admitted, against it, but that does not go further back than the fifth century ; and the suppression of the name *Jesus* would be the natural result of the reverence which never suffered a name that had been common among Jews to become common among Christians. The reading in question has been adopted, on critical grounds, by Fritzsche and Meyer, and was received at one time by Tischendorf. As has been said before, there *must* have been some other name besides the patronymic.

Note 5, p. 79.

" But Dysmas, then some eighteen winters old,
   Begged hard for mercy."

The name is taken from the apocryphal Gospel of Nicodemus, c. x. ; the story from the Arabic collection of legends known as the *Gospel of the Infancy*, c. xxiii.

GOMER.

Note I, p. 87.

"And so I wooed thee, and thou didst not spurn
The prophet's offered love."

I follow Dr. Pusey (*Minor Prophets*, p. 8) and Ewald (*Propheten*, i. p. 126) in looking at the strange history of these chapters as no parable or allegory, but the story of an actual life, the education by which the prophet was led to apprehend the mysteries of God's dealings with Israel.

In the absence of any *data* as to the previous life of Gomer, I have assumed that here, as throughout the history of Israel, the two sins of idolatry and sensual licence were closely intertwined. The Ashtaroth worship in groves, which Jezebel had introduced into the northern kingdom, had brought with it all the abominations of Phœnician worship ; and it would not be too much to say that every harlot in Israel was probably a votary of the goddess. Comp. Hosea iv. 13, 14.

THE HOUSE OF THE RECHABITES.

Note 1, p. 102.

" We rode together, I, the Kenite chief."

The connection of the clan or sect of the Rechabites with the Kenites who had taken part in the conquest of Canaan under Hobab, and who continued to live among the Canaanites, retaining their old nomadic life, is distinctly stated in 1 Chron. ii. 55 : " The Kenites that came of Hemath, the father of the house of Rechab."

It is interesting from this point of view to think of the strange union of zeal and dissimulation in Jonadab, as transmitted from the great Kenite heroine, the wife of Heber.

Note 2, p. 103.

——— *"A whisper runs
(I know it) that some dreamer in his cell,
Who counts himself a prophet, has condemned
That deed of vengeance."*

This is, I think, hardly more than a legitimate inference from the language of Hosea i. 4.　He could say, in "the word of the Lord," "I will avenge the blood of Jezreel upon the house of Jehu," though Jehu had been the instrument of a righteous retribution.　He could hardly fail to have condemned also the falsehood and the cruelty which mixed itself with his zeal in the slaughter of the Baal worshippers. And if this were so in the time of Jeroboam the Second, it is probable enough that some such testimony had been borne at an earlier period by some member of the prophetic order to which Hosea belonged.

Note 3, p. 105.

" ' Sons of the chariot of our Israel's strength.' "

The close resemblance between the name Rechab and *Recheb* (the " chariot"), applied to Elijah (2 Kings ii. 12) and Elisha (2 Kings xiii. 14), suggests the thought that the name, "sons of Rechab," was chosen rather than "sons of Jonadab," for the sake of a *paronomasia*, such as the Hebrew mind always delighted in.

Note 4, p. 111.

" ' The son of Rechab shall not want a man
To stand before my face for evermore.' "

The word rendered "to stand before" is, with the addition "before the Lord," all but essentially liturgical. It is used of the Levites (Deut. x. 8 ; xviii. 5, 7), of the worship of the Patriarchs (Gen. xix. 27), of the priests (1 Kings viii. 11 ; 2 Chron. xxix. 11 ; Nehem. vii. 65), of prophets (1 Kings xviii. 15), of priests and Levites together (Ps. cxxxiv. 1 ; cxxxv. 2).

Note 5, p. 112.

" And, when they bid us, in their mirth and pride,
Sing at their feasts the chief of Zion's songs."

The following *data* will justify this assumption :—

(1.) If adopted into the tribe of Levi, the prominent work of the Rechabites would be to take part in the minstrelsy of the Temple.

Q

(2.) The Latin rendering of the proper names in 1 Chron. ii. 55, as *"canentes et resonantes,"* indicates a Jewish tradition in the time of Jerome, that the Rechabites were famous for their musical skill.

(3.) The heading of Ps. lxxi. in the Septuagint version as composed or sung "by the sons of Jonadab, the first that were carried away captive," shows that the pressure of the captivity fell heaviest on them.

(4.) On their return from the captivity they are found in close connection with the Netophathites (1 Chron. ii. 54, 55); and in the villages of the Netophathites dwelt "the sons of the singers" (Nehem. xii. 28).

(5.) I venture to think that the fierce burning zeal which almost startles us in this Psalm ("Happy shall he be that taketh thy little ones and dasheth them against the stones") is more characteristic of the Kenite than the Israelite Psalmists.

Note 6, p. 113.

" Thou still shalt stand, and for thy people pray,
Thy grey hairs crowned with glory."

Compare 2 Macc. xiii. 14:—"There appeared a man with grey hairs, and exceeding glorious, who was of a wonderful and excellent majesty. Then Onias answered and said, 'This is a lover of the brethren, who prayeth much for the people and for the Holy City, to wit, Jeremias, the prophet of God.'"

Note 1, p. 128.

——" *He who knew*
The depths of Islam."

Islam—resignation, submission to the will of God—was proclaimed by Mahomet as the one essential religion, which had
been inherited from the patriarchs, preached by the prophets,
and revived by himself as its new and greatest apostle. Comp.
Koran, ch. ii. & iii. (Sale's *Translation*); or ch. xci. & xcvii.
(Rodwell's).

"They who set their face with resignation Godward and do
what is right, their reward is with the Lord."

"When his Lord said to Abraham, 'Resign thyself to me,' he
said, 'I resign myself to the Lord of the Worlds.'"

"And this to his children did Abraham bequeath, and Jacob
also, saying, 'O, my children! truly God hath chosen a religion
for you; so die not unless ye also be Muslims'" (*sc.*, resigned).
(Rodwell, xci.)

Note 2, p. 130.

" *It passed into a proverb—'Ka'ab's deed*
Of noble goodness :—There is none like that.' "

The story is given by Kallius in his notes to Rostgaard's translation of the collection of proverbs known as *Arabum Philosophia
Popularis*, p. 57. The current form of the proverb is that Arabs,
in speaking of any one whose nobleness they wish to praise,
describe him as "more generous than Ka'ab." See also Pocock,
Hist. Arab., p. 344.

RIZPAH THE DAUGHTER OF AIAH.

Note I, p. 147.

" *That song of the Bow re-echoed.*"

I follow some of the best critics in this interpretation of the words, which stand in the authorised version as "Also he bade them teach the children of Judah *the use of* the bow," 2 Sam. i. 18. The words in italics are, as the italics show, an interpolation, and they obscure the sense. What was meant was, that the song of which the "bow of Jonathan" was the central point, was that which David taught the children of Judah to sing.

Note 2, p. 151.

" *The Urim's mysterious glow.*"

Out of the many conflicting conjectures as to the nature and mode of use of the Urim and Thummim, I have chosen, not as in itself most probable, but as fittest for employment here, the tradition given by Epiphanius, that it was a diamond which, according to the light which it shot forth, red, or clear, or dim, indicated bloodshed, or prosperity, or disaster.

THE SONG OF DEBÔRAH.

Note I, p. 168.

*" Then, at length, new chieftains they chose, as Gods to guide and
to save."*

"They chose new gods." It can hardly, I think, admit of
question that the word *Elohim* here, as in Exod. xxi. 6 ; xxii. 9 ;
Ps. lxxxii. 1, 6, is used of the judges and rulers of Israel. The
whole order of thought is broken if we suppose Debôrah to be
speaking of the lapse of the people into idolatry, not of the
revival of true life and energy, as subsequent to the time when
she "arose, a mother in Israel."

It seems worth while to submit to those who are conversant
with such matters, whether this frequent occurrence of the word
Elohim in its lower sense, in the earlier history of Israel, and the
consequent necessity which there must have been for the loftier
and more distinctive name, has had its due weight in the Elohistic
and Jehovistic controversies which have vexed us during the last
few years. Here, in a poem which bears in its minutest details
the stamp of the remote antiquity to which it is ascribed, the two
words are placed in direct antithesis with each other ; and this is
surely incompatible with any hypothesis which sees in the occurrence of the name Jehovah in any book, or portion of a book, a
proof that it originated after the influence of Samuel had changed
the religious nomenclature of the people.

Note 2, p. 169.

"*From the lips of those who rejoice at eve round the wells cool and calm.*"

The verse is not an easy one, but the literal rendering would, I believe, run thus : " From the voice of those who divide" (but uncertain whether they divide the spoil, as in Ps. lxviii. 12, or count their flocks) "between the places of drawing water." In either case what is described is the joy of victory.

Note 3, p. 169.

"*Lead forth thy conquered, thy captives, marching in triumph along.*"

The phrase of "leading captivity captive" has become so familiar to us in its rhetorical use, that we forget that the repetition of a word from the same root does but emphasize the fact, not that the conquerors are conquered, but that the captives are taken.

Note 4, p. 170.

"*True stock of the heroes of old who fighting with Amalek died.*"

Here again it will be best to give a literal prose rendering, "From Ephraim, a root of them in (or against) Amalek." The question is, what is meant by the last two words? By some critics (Michaelis) they are referred to the battle with the Amalekites in Exod. xvii. 8—16, in which Joshua, the leader of Ephraim, commanded the army of Israel. This, however, seems very improbable. Ewald, adopting the local meaning ("in Amalek"), gives up all attempt at accounting for the limitation. A comparison of one or two passages may perhaps explain it. There was a district in the tribe of Ephraim known as the Mount of the Amalekites (Judg. xii. 15), and so called probably as having once been conquered or occupied by them. The period to which this may be referred is beyond question the time when the Amalekites, in conjunction with the Moabites under Eglon, conquered Jericho, and established themselves on the west side of the Jordan (Judg. iii. 13, 14). There can be as little doubt that the victory which dispossessed them, and to which Debôrah referred as still fresh in the memory of the people, was won when Ehud "blew a trumpet in *the mountain of Ephraim*, and the children of Israel went down with him from the mountain" (Judg. iii. 27). It is surprising that a coincidence which lies so near the surface should have escaped the notice of so acute a writer as Ewald.

Note 5, p. 172.

"*Kishon, the onward-rushing.*"

I follow Ewald in adopting this rather than "*ancient*" as the true rendering. It is at once nearer to the primitive meaning of the root, and more in harmony with the context.

Note 6, p. 172.

"*The word from the Prophet's lips came.*"

In the absence of any record of a visible appearance of an angel, in the later sense of the term, it is allowable to take the neutral word "messenger," as applied to a prophet of the Lord. Perhaps, as in Malachi (ii. 7), it was used specially of a *priestly* prophet. (Comp. also Eccles. v. 6.)

Note 7, p. 174.

"*The costliest robes of their priests.*"

I have ventured on an interpolation here, but it is, I believe, one which may be legitimately inferred from the context. The mother of Sisera was expecting her son's army to return laden with spoil, especially from Ephraim. That spoil would have included the plunder of the Tabernacle at Shiloh, and the richest prizes there would have been the vestments of the priesthood, on the embroidery of which, and (so far as we know) on that alone, the skill and industry of the women of Israel were exercised. The "broidered coat of gold, and blue, and scarlet, and purple, and fine linen" (Exod. xxviii. 6), exactly answers to "the divers colours of needlework" which the inmates of Sisera's harem were expecting.

THE EARLIEST CHRISTIAN HYMN.

Note 1, p. 175.

There are no special points, it is believed, in this poem re-
quiring explanation, but it may be well to say a few words on the
Hymn itself. It occurs at the end of an Ethical Guide to Life
which Clement of Alexandria wrote under the title of the *Pædagôgus*, or Tutor.* The central thought of the whole is that
Christ is the true Pædagôgus, the guardian, teacher, friend ; and
this is worked out with every possible variety of illustration, and
applied to the details of daily life. At the end, after a prayer of
wonderful beauty, he burst out into a kind of choral, dithyrambic
ode, in anapæstic metre, the lines very short and abrupt, and the
whole being more exclamatory and fervid than most later hymns.
Its chief interest lies in its being almost the only surviving relic
of a class of hymns which would perhaps seem startling to us, but
which were the natural aftergrowth of the ecstatic doxologies,
the "spiritual songs," that formed part at least of the working
of the Gift of Tongues (comp. Nitzsch, *Christliche Lehre*,
ii. p. 268).

* Impossible as it is to express the exact idea in English, this word perhaps
comes nearer than any other.

₊ It is right to state, that the substance of many of these
notes has already appeared in Dr. Smith's *Dictionary of the
Bible*, and is reproduced, in its present form, by Mr. Murray's
kind permission.

R